PUFFIN BOOKS

Editor : Kaye Webb

PS 198

MULBRIDGE MANOR

When a poet writes an adventure story something magical happens, quite ordinary events take on an extra quality of wonder, and quite ordinary people become fascinating or mysterious. For a poet's gift is to see everything as if it were happening for the first time, so that everything he writes about, places and people, is fresh and brilliant.

In *Mulbridge Manor* James Reeves tells us the story of how Richard Masters and his friends hunt for a missing will, in order to save old Miss Matilda Jay from losing her home. He tells of their clash with two shady gentlemen called Seedy and Dusty, and of how, even after the will has been found, the danger is not over. But he also makes the children themselves separate and interesting characters, and throughout the book there is the feeling of a golden summer in the best sort of country, with warm drowsy days and eventful moonlit nights. In fact he combines gaiety and excitement and poetry together, in a story which will delight boys and girls from 9 upwards.

Among other books by James Reeves are *Pigeons and Princesses*, *The Wandering Moon*, and *The Blackbird in the Lilac*.

Cover illustration by Geraldine Spence

The search was going to be a long business (*page 48*)

JAMES REEVES

Mulbridge Manor

——————— ✳ ———————

Illustrated by Geraldine Spence

PENGUIN BOOKS

Penguin Books Ltd, Harmondsworth, Middlesex
AUSTRALIA: Penguin Books Pty Ltd, 762 Whitehorse Road,
Mitcham, Victoria

—

First published by Heinemann 1958
Published in Puffin Books 1963

—

Copyright © James Reeves, 1958
Illustrations copyright © William Heinemann Ltd, 1958

—

Made and printed in Great Britain
by Richard Clay & Company Ltd,
Bungay, Suffolk
Set in Monotype Garamond

Contents

Chapter One

A TENNIS-BALL GOES
TRESPASSING

IT was a Wednesday afternoon, about tea-time, in early August. Mulcaster, an ancient city near the south coast, was a sleepy place at the best of times. Today, when the shops were shut, and many of the citizens away on holiday, it was lifeless and deserted. The bells in the cathedral tower dropped four notes on the silent air, almost apologetically, as if sorry to disturb the city in its sleep. The old red roofs looked baked in the hot sun. The blinds of the shops were down. The new paint on some of the shutters was already blistered with heat.

Up North Street, through the sleeping town, toiled a boy on a bicycle – or rather, a boy and a girl on a bicycle, *one* bicycle, not two; and it was not a tandem either; it was an ordinary boy's bicycle, not a very new one, and the chain and the saddle-spring creaked under the weight of a quite big boy and a quite small girl.

Not only did the bicycle carry a boy and a girl, it carried also a small cricket bat and a big tea-basket. It was no wonder that the springs complained.

'Quarter past four,' said the boy between puffs, as he heard the cathedral bell. 'Better get a move on. They'll be waiting.'

Richard Masters was a serious boy of twelve. He was at a prep school and therefore pretty important, but of course he was on holiday at present. Most of his friends were away at the sea. Dr Masters, his father, was taking his holiday in September. That is why Richard and his sister Cherry were at home this boiling August day. From Richard's point of view there were two things wrong with Cherry. She was a girl, and she was only half his age. But she adored her brother, which was some compensation, so that he grudgingly forgave her for being no good at throwing a cricket ball, not interested in stamp collecting, and a bit of a nuisance when he wanted to be off on his own. Today he had agreed to play with Cherry, there being very little else to do. His parents did not like him to take her on the carrier of his bicycle, but he refused to play with her on any other terms. As Richard's mother kept telling herself, Richard was a sensible and serious boy and could fairly be trusted to run no risks.

Cherry was silent, enjoying the ride. Grimly she clutched hold of Richard's saddle, as instructed. Occasionally she caught her breath as the cycle wobbled, but for the most part she was only too happy to be on her adored brother's carrier. She hardly noticed how it cut into her small legs. Instead, perfectly confident in Richard's skill as a cyclist, she was able to look round her at the silent shops, the corn-merchant's brown dog dozing on the pavement, the grey parrot in old Mrs O'Grady's window. Usually she was talkative – Cherry, that is to say, not the parrot – but she knew her talking got on Richard's nerves, and talking was absolutely forbidden while cycling. She hardly opened her mouth once in fifty yards.

On the outskirts of the town they stopped outside a house, and Richard tinkled his bell. But there was no need for this. The Jones children were already waiting. They too had bicycles and a picnic basket.

Richard and Cherry dismounted – or rather, Richard dismounted, and Cherry fell off.

'Hullo, Winston,' Cherry said. 'Did you remember to bring the ball?'

'Hullo, kid,' said Winston Jones. He did not condescend to answer Cherry's question. He was nearly as old as Richard.

'Ready?' asked Winston, addressing Richard. 'Let's go.'

Deborah, his sister, older than he by two years, made a moaning sound.

'My tyre's flat,' she said. 'I thought I'd pumped it up. In fact, I *did* pump it up, but it's come unpumped.'

'Here,' said Richard politely but with some impatience, 'let me do it.'

He unclipped his pump and screwed it to the wheel of Deborah's cycle.

'Thought so,' he said. 'Valve's loose. Never mind. That'll hold up till we get there.'

They proceeded as fast as the heat of the afternoon and the slight upward slope of the road would let them.

Soon the town was left behind. A few cottages

lined the road, a farmstead, a petrol station. The great
elm trees at the edges of the road gave them some
shade, but not much, for the sun was high in the
cloudless blue sky.

Nobody spoke. For one thing, it is not easy to have
a conversation on bicycles. For another, cycling took
all their energy. There was no need to discuss their
route; everybody knew where they were bound for.

Mulbridge Heath is a wild, open space two or three
miles outside the city. Acres and acres of grassland
stretch away across the high ground and down to the
valley where the farm tracks lead eventually to the
village of Mulbridge. Part of the heath is covered
with brambles, fine for blackberrying in September;
part of it is overgrown with bracken; there are few big
trees, but many stunted saplings and bushes. There
are rabbit-warrens and mole-colonies by the hundred.
On the far side there is a wide open space, perfect for
races and ball games, where the grass is short and
springy, and there are few bushes. The heath is
crossed by two or three tracks on which the marks of
horses' hooves are usually to be seen. Butterflies float
lazily about the gorse bushes, and even in August the
birds are never silent.

Along one edge of the open space is a long, high
wall of old red brick. This contains the grounds of
Mulbridge Manor. Except on Bank Holidays and at
week-ends the whole heath is almost deserted. Past
the farther edge of the Manor grounds runs a road of
yellow gravel, hard and smooth, but so little used that
it has never been covered with tar and granite-chips –
'metalled', as it is called. As it crosses the heath, it is
bordered only by dry ditches, but over towards Mulbridge it drops down between thorn hedges; a mile

from Mulbridge the famous Mulbridge Woods begin, famous for their many birds, their primroses, and their bluebells. These woods have been made a bird sanctuary, where no bird may be killed and no nest robbed; and the birds express their gratitude by singing morning, noon, and evening, and making the cool shady depths ring with melody.

The three bicycles arrived on Mulbridge Heath, and the riders dismounted and lay on the soft turf. Everything was so peaceful that not even Cherry spoke for perhaps three minutes.

'I want my tea,' she said at last.

Tea and French cricket was the programme. There was something of an argument as to which should come first. Cherry and Winston strongly favoured beginning with tea. Richard wanted a short game first. Deborah favoured neither. All she wanted to do was to lie in the sun and think deliciously of nothing.

'You vote for tea, Deborah, don't you?' Winston appealed to her.

'Oughtn't we to wait for Anne?' said Deborah dreamily.

'Not coming,' said Winston. 'At least not till later. Her mother's ill again, and she's got to stay home and help.'

'Poor Anne,' said Cherry. 'I *wish* she could come.'

'Perhaps she will,' said Deborah. 'Anyway, she knows where we are. We're to stay here till at least six. Have you got a watch, Richard?'

'Yes,' said Richard. 'Well, come on: if you lazy lubbers won't stir your stumps, we'd better have tea.'

There was no further opposition. They moved into the narrow line of shade afforded by the Manor wall, squatted down, and opened their baskets.

'Here you are, Cherry,' said Richard. 'Potted meat or currant bun?'

'Potted meat,' said Cherry. 'I love potted meat. Mummy doesn't. Does your Mummy like potted meat, Winston?'

'How should I know?' asked Winston loftily, his mouth full of banana sandwich.

Deborah poured out orange-squash for her brother and herself. They had brought a collapsible green plastic cup and an enamel mug. Richard and Cherry had fizzy lemonade. After a certain amount of swopping, everyone settled down to munch happily. Cake followed sandwiches and buns, and biscuits followed the cake. The chocolate biscuits were already melting with the heat. Cherry was soon smeared with milk chocolate. Richard had brought plums to finish with, and these attracted a wasp. No one was stung, but there was considerable disturbance. Deborah screamed.

'Oh, kill it, Winston!' she said. 'Kill it! I hate wasps!'

'You ought to love animals,' said Cherry righteously.

'Wasps aren't animals,' said Deborah stoutly.

'Well, what *are* they?' said Cherry.

'Insects,' said Richard, as if that settled the question.

'Wasps are a darned nuisance,' said Winston, defending his sister.

Presently the wasp lost interest, and all was peace once more. Winston began seeing how far he could spit plum-stones. Cherry discovered, when all the plums were eaten, that she was to be married in rags. Two white butterflies chased one another over the Manor wall. A plane flew overhead, very high and almost out of sight.

'Jet,' said Winston, scarcely raising his head, and

speaking through a bun he had started eating as an afterthought.

Richard methodically tidied up the paper bags, got up, and said: 'Come on. What about this game of French cricket? We'll *never* get started.'

'O.K., chief,' said Winston, jumping up very promptly for one who had eaten so many sandwiches and buns.

'Where's the ball, Deborah? Don't say you've lost it.'

'I'll bowl first.'

'Can I bat first? Oh, please can I bat first, Richard?'

'Oh, all right.'

Richard handed Cherry the bat. The others spread out. Winston bowled, very gently. No one could have missed it but Cherry. Deborah, standing behind her, was dreaming, partly about rabbits, and partly about her favourite subject – nothing. The ball bounced up against her knee.

'Bowl!' shouted Richard. 'For goodness' sake, bowl. It's your turn. That's right. Out!'

'Oh, I *wasn't*!' said Cherry, her eyes beginning to fill with tears.

'Oh, all right,' said Richard hastily. 'Have another chance. But mind, next time you're really out.'

So the game went on. Richard went in, scoring uncountable runs and sending the fielders in all directions over the grassy heath. Then it was Winston's turn, neatly bowled by a cunning lob from Richard. Richard's second innings was unexpectedly ended by a lucky ball from Deborah. Now it was her turn to bat.

Deborah was not good at ball games. Her dark hair got in her eyes; her long legs got into her own and everybody else's way. Her arms and hands seemed all

joints, and never did what she wanted them to. Nevertheless, she was desperately eager to make a big score. She held the bat resolutely in front of her legs and faced the bowler. It was Winston. He threw hard. Deborah did absolutely nothing except close her eyes and the ball was fielded by Richard. Deborah turned and faced Richard. He threw, and she hit the ball a fair distance. She was so surprised that she forgot to swing the bat round her and score.

Cherry scampered off after the ball. She threw, and it did not even reach Deborah. Winston intervened, and bowled a second time. Once again Deborah

missed, and Richard fielded. This time Deborah was
determined not only to hit the ball, but also to score.
She raised the bat, closed her eyes, swiped madly, and
hit the ball square in the middle of the bat.

'Oh, well *done*!' shrieked Cherry.

Everyone gazed up at the rising tennis-ball. Then,
almost simultaneously, everyone said, 'Oh.'

Deborah, remembering this time to score, had made
five runs before the ball dropped out of sight behind
the red brick wall of the Manor grounds.

'Sister,' said Winston, 'in the words of the poet,
you've sure gone and done it.'

Everyone seemed to agree with the poet.

'Here, help me up, someone,' said Richard, 'and I'll see if I can see it.'

With the help of Winston he scrambled high enough up the wall to look over the top. In the tangled meadow that lay inside the wall there was no hope of catching sight of the lost ball. Except for an old horse lazily cropping the rank grass, not a living creature was in sight. Richard sprang to the ground.

'Better have a council of war,' he said, 'and decide what's to be done. It's our only ball. We haven't got another. We must get it back somehow.'

Chapter Two

SCATTY MATTY

ANNE SHIPLEY was nine. She was alone with her mother in their tiny cottage in Mulbridge. Mr and Mrs Shipley were Londoners, but they had moved to the pleasant village of Mulbridge because of Mrs Shipley's health. She had a weak chest, and when it was bad she suffered a good deal. Mr Shipley was a house-painter. Just now, unfortunately, he was away on a job in Portsmouth. He was obliged to stay away when his firm was at work a long distance from home; for you cannot get from Mulbridge to Portsmouth and back every day. It was unfortunate because, just now, Mrs Shipley had a bad cough. But it was the school holiday, and Anne could do nearly everything that had to be done in the house. This fine August morning she had made her mother stay in bed.

'I can do everything,' she said, '*easily*.'

She scarcely thought of her plan to go picnicking on the heath with her school friends, Winston and Deborah Jones and their Mulcaster friends, Richard and Cherry Masters. Perhaps she would be able to leave her mother after tea and go to the heath for an hour before bed-time.

Anne was one of the most practical people of nine you can possibly imagine. She lit the paraffin cooking-stove – they had no gas and the Shipleys could not afford electricity – and boiled a kettle for tea. Then she cut some bread, got out the breakfast cereal, sugar, butter, marmalade, and all the necessary knives, spoons, and crockery. She laid the breakfast tray with extreme care, made the tea, and, when all was ready, took it in to her mother.

Poor Mrs Shipley had had a bad night, coughing continually and keeping herself awake most of the time. She looked tired. When Anne appeared with the breakfast tray, she said all the usual things that mothers say on such occasions: she was an angel (though how an angel could possibly have brought in the breakfast tray Anne could never understand); what her mother would do without her, her mother could not possibly imagine.

'How do you feel, Mummy?' asked Anne.

'Not so bad, my dear,' said Mrs Shipley, 'but I've been coughing a lot.'

'Had I better get the doctor?'

'No, I'll just stay in bed, if you can manage, sweetheart. That always does me good. If I don't get better, I'll have the doctor again when Daddy gets back.'

'All right, Mummy. Now don't talk any more, but

have some tea while it's hot. I'll get my breakfast in
the kitchen.'

When Anne came in for the tray, her mother said:

'I don't like you staying in on a lovely day like this,
just to look after me. I can manage all right. I'll get
up in half an hour.'

'You'll do nothing of the sort,' said Anne firmly.
'Getting up now would be the death of you. Good
job it's summer and we needn't light the boiler. Now
just you snuggle down, and I'll get on with the washing up and the house, and after that I'll go shopping.'

Then she paused.

'Oh,' she said.

'What is it, dear?'

'Nothing, Mummy – nothing at all. There – let me
put the pillow right and make you comfy.'

But she had remembered her appointment with the
others. She had better send a message to tell them not
to expect her. Mrs Robins was going into Mulcaster
that morning, she knew, and Mrs Robins was a friend
of hers. She would get her to deliver a message at the
Joneses. That was settled.

Then she finished washing-up, made her bed, and
did a bit of dusting, not very thoroughly, but well
enough, she thought. She could never see the point
of dusting. Things got just as bad next day; still,
Mummy always did it, so she had better do the same.

At last she was ready to go out. She went in to her
mother, found out what they needed from the village,
saw that the invalid was comfortable, and set out.

She took her big doll's pram, but with only a very
small doll in it, as most of the space would be needed
for bread, flour, sausages, apples, and various other
purchases. She was lucky enough to meet her friend

Mrs Robins in the little post office, which also served as a sweet and cigarette shop, a paper shop, and a general meeting-place for everyone to have a good chatter, and exchange gossip, news, and complaints. Mrs Robins promised faithfully to call on the Joneses. It would be a chance to have a nice talk with Mrs Jones about everybody's illnesses and where everyone had gone for their holidays.

So the day went on. How quickly time passed! No sooner had Anne got back with the shopping than it was time to get on with lunch; no sooner had she washed up after lunch, than it was time to feed the hens, wash a few clothes – mainly some summer dresses belonging to her dolls, which, she admitted, were in a disgraceful condition – and begin thinking about tea.

By tea-time Mrs Shipley was better. She had slept most of the afternoon, and had not coughed at all.

'I'll get up now,' she said, 'and you can go out and play for a bit.'

'You're not to get up,' Anne told her mother. 'I'll go up to the heath and play for a bit if you *promise* on your honour – cross your heart! – *not* to get out of bed whatever happens – even if the roof falls in.'

Her mother laughed, and promised – cross her heart. So after tea Anne once more saw that her mother was comfortable and then set off to meet her friends.

It was about this time that the four others rose from their council of war under the wall of Mulbridge Manor. They had decided what to do.

The difficulty was a peculiar one. It was, in fact, Scatty Matty.

Everybody called her Scatty Matty. Her full name was Miss Matilda Jay; and since the death of her brother earlier that year, she had lived alone at the Manor. Old Stephen Jay had been a curious man, fond of the country, fond of books, never stirring from his beloved Manor except on an occasional business visit to Mulcaster. Matilda, his sister, who kept house for him, was seen abroad much oftener; everybody knew she was harmless, yet all the children were a little scared. They didn't know what to make of her. They supposed she was rather grand and stand-offish. Then she had such an odd reputation. She was always doing strange things – nothing special, and certainly nothing to anybody's harm; but somehow an old lady who might walk out with a sunshade in December or bicycle dangerously along the country lanes wobbling violently from side to side, or go into the chemist's for two nice lamb chops – well, such a lady was not altogether to be trusted.

It was no joke, the children felt, going boldly up to the front door and asking Scatty Matty if they might look for a ball in her meadow. Anything might happen. Nevertheless, somebody had to go.

'After all,' said Winston, who had given the matter deep thought, 'she can't eat us.'

Nobody seemed inclined to agree.

'You go, then, Winston,' said his sister.

'O.K.,' said Winston. 'Coming, Richard?'

The two boys set off together. They skirted the wall until they came to the big stone gate-posts with the lions on top, one on each side, and here they left Deborah and Cherry. The gates were always open. Indeed, they were so rusty, and the grass in the drive had grown up so thickly around them, that it looked as if they had not been shut for a century. While the boys marched steadily down the centre of the drive towards the old red brick mansion, Deborah began to imagine the smart carriages drawn by pairs of glossy black horses which might have driven through those gates in the old days.

At the front door Winston hesitated a moment, and then gave the iron bell-pull a tug. Seconds later, and miles away, it seemed, a faint bell jangled. A dog barked. That would be the old half-blind, black retriever that sometimes followed Miss Jay when she went out.

At last Scatty Matty herself stood in the doorway.

'Please,' said Richard.

Matty was of middle height, rather thin, and dressed in an odd assortment of things that looked as if they had come from a church jumble sale. Some of them, in fact, had. But her grey hair was very tidy, and her eyes and cheeks were bright.

'Yes?' she said.

'Please,' repeated Richard, speaking rather quietly from nervousness, 'we've lost our ball in your meadow and we want your permission to look for it, if you would be so kind.'

Matty shook her head.

'I'm awfully sorry,' she said. 'I never go to whist-drives now. I gave it up when my brother died. But I'll take a ticket if I can find my purse. Lie down, Dennis! The gentleman won't hurt you.'

This was addressed to the old retriever, who was growling suspiciously and advancing upon the boys. The dog obeyed. Richard explained again, louder. Nobody had known that Scatty Matty was rather deaf. Perhaps this was why she seemed aloof and haughty. Deaf people often seem so, until you get to know them.

When she understood that they wanted to look for their ball, not to sell tickets for a whist-drive, she smiled kindly and nodded her head with vigour.

'But of course,' she said. 'Go anywhere you like. Have a jolly good look. You may find all sorts of things in the paddock, for I'm always losing this and that. Don't mind Dragon. He wouldn't harm a fly.

If you find my gardening gloves, be sure to bring them back, will you? I lost them last week. But I'm afraid Dragon will have eaten them by now. I said he wouldn't harm a *fly*, but I don't think he's so reliable with gloves. So long for now.'

Before the boys could thank her, she smiled again, withdrew into the house and closed the door.

'Rather a gracious lady, if you ask me,' said Richard, beginning to think they had been wrong about Miss Jay.

'Rum old girl,' said Winston. 'What does she keep a dragon for?'

'That will be the horse,' said Richard.

As it turned out, he was right, as usual. They went back and told the girls. All four went to the overgrown meadow which Matty had called 'the paddock' and began searching. Dragon eyed them casually and went on cropping the rank grass. Deborah tired of looking for the ball and went to talk to him. How she wished she had a lump of sugar or a carrot! And wouldn't it be wonderful to climb on his back and take a ride?

Within ten minutes Cherry and the others had found not only a pair of gardening gloves, but also a big hair-comb, a silver pencil, a rusty kitchen-knife, and a key-ring with a key on it. The only thing they could not find, it seemed, was the ball.

The search went on. Richard climbed the wall, with Winston's help, in order to decide where the ball had gone over. Just as he had made up his mind, he caught sight of Anne coming over the heath.

'Hullo, Anne!' he called. 'Come round and help look for the ball! When you get to the corner of the wall, follow it round and it brings you to the gates. Go and meet Anne, Cherry Blossom, there's a good girl!'

Cherry ran to meet their friend.

'Deborah hit the ball over,' she explained. 'It was a jolly good swipe. We've been looking for ages. Scatty Matty said we could. The horse is called Dragon. Is your mummy better?'

So she prattled on till they reached the scene of the search.

'Where did you lose it, Richard?' asked Anne.

'If I knew that,' said Richard scornfully, 'I wouldn't still be looking for it, would I? About where you're standing, I should say.'

Anne bent down and picked something up from the centre of a clump of dock-leaves.

'Is this the one?' she asked.

'Yes,' said Richard. 'Well done, I must say.'

'Found it?' said Winston. 'Good show! Let's get on with the game. Come on, kids.'

'I don't want to play any more,' said Cherry. 'Do you want to play, Anne?'

'I don't mind,' said Anne. 'What a lovely house, isn't it? I *do* wish we could look all round it. Do you think she'd mind?'

'No, we can't go sneaking about like that,' said Richard firmly. 'Perhaps she'll ask us. Anyway, we'd better take all these things back. She'll be glad to have the gloves.'

Deborah was roused from her rapt contemplation of the old horse, and joined the others on their way back to the house.

Once more Winston pulled the rusty bell-handle, and once more Dennis growled from the depths. Cherry trembled.

'Oo-er!' she said apprehensively, hiding behind Richard.

When Miss Jay came to the door, Richard politely handed her the gloves, the comb, the pencil, the knife, and the key-ring.

'Thank you very much,' he said, remembering to speak up. 'We found the ball all right, and we found these too.'

Miss Jay was delighted, especially with the gardening gloves.

'How very good of you,' she said. 'But what a lot of you there are, all of a sudden! There were only two of you just now, weren't there?'

Nobody said anything, and the three girls looked sheepish.

'But never mind,' Matty went on. 'I think you must have a reward for finding all these things. I think I have some oranges and plums, even if I haven't any lemonade. And perhaps there's a biscuit or two. What do you say, Dennis?'

'I hope the old girl isn't going to give us dog-biscuits,' said Winston to himself. Dennis wagged his tail in an encouraging way.

'Good,' said Matty. 'Then come along in, all of you. We'll go into the dining-room, shall we?'

'It's very kind of you,' Richard said.

'Oh, thank you,' said Deborah.

Anne squeezed Cherry's hand excitedly. They were actually going into the Manor.

'Follow me, everyone,' went on Matty. 'Make yourselves at home while I find the refreshments.'

Then she turned round rather unexpectedly and paused.

'There's something,' she added – 'there's something I particularly want to talk to you about. It's *most* particular.'

Chapter Three

THE WILL

So impressive was Miss Jay's tone of voice as she said, 'Something most particular,' that the children almost forgot about the refreshments in their curiosity to know what the 'something' could be. But they were obliged to be patient. They followed her into the dining-room and sat down, while she rummaged in the sideboard and brought out a tin of biscuits and some plates. Then she wandered off, followed by the black retriever, in search of oranges.

They had time to look round the room. It was long, low, and rather dark. This was not because there were few windows, but because the heavy panelling gave the room an air of gloom, almost of mystery. Deborah was already imagining secret doors behind sliding panels, passages leading down dark stairways to a hidden opening in the cliff – except that the cliffs were many miles away, far off beyond Mulcaster. The furniture too was dark and heavy. A huge sideboard stood against one wall, with branched silver candlesticks on it and pewter and earthenware mugs hanging from hooks in a dresser behind it. The room was a little musty, as if it were no longer used; perhaps Miss Jay had her meals in the kitchen.

The children spoke little, for they were awed by the strangeness and gloom of their new surroundings. Even Cherry was silent.

Presently Matty reappeared with some oranges and a great bowl full of plums. She passed the biscuits round, and the fruit, and told the children to eat all they wanted. The biscuits were rather soft, and the oranges were rather dry. Only the plums, from the trees in the Manor orchard, were fresh and juicy. But no one ate much.

'I am so very grateful to you all,' said Matty at last, 'for finding all those things for me. The gardening gloves are so useful. I have no one to help with the garden, and I have to do what I can myself. The silver pencil must have been my brother's. As for the key, I can't think what it fits; but that's no matter. I'm awfully glad you found your ball.'

'It was very kind of you –' began Richard.

'Not at all, not at all,' said Matty. 'We like visitors, don't we, Dennis? We get so few nowadays.'

Dennis said he wasn't sure, but Matty took no notice.

'Which of you is the eldest?' she asked.

'Deborah is,' said Richard. 'Deborah Jones, her name is. But she's rather dreamy.'

Deborah drew a deep breath, as if she was going to deny the accusation, thought better of it and remained silent.

'And what is *your* name?' asked Matty, turning to Richard.

'Richard Masters, and this is my sister Cherry.'

'Oh, indeed? Then I shall call you Richard. I can't call you Master Masters, can I? Besides, nobody bothers about those things any more.'

'This is Winston Jones,' Richard went on. 'He's Deborah's brother.'

'Good afternoon, Winston,' said Matty. 'I am very glad to know you.'

'Same here, ma'am,' said Winston.

'And this is Anne Shipley. We all live in Mulcaster except Anne; she comes from Mulbridge.'

'Would you all like to see over the Manor?' asked Matty.

The children all began to give signs of excitement and curiosity, but Matty went on: 'Not today, though. Tomorrow perhaps. You see, it is getting late, and I have something very particular to say to you all. When is your bed-time, Cherry? I expect you will have to get home soon.'

'She's supposed to go at six o'clock,' explained Richard.

'Oh, I'm *not*, Richard,' said Cherry emphatically. 'Not in the holidays, and in summer time especially.'

'Well, she oughtn't to be much longer, Miss Jay,' said Richard.

'Then if you've all had enough refreshments, we'll go into the library. It'll be better there. Follow me, please, all of you.'

Their disappointment at not seeing over the house immediately was overcome by renewed curiosity to know what Matty had to say. They got up promptly and followed her.

The children's idea of a library was for the most part vague in the extreme. Richard's school had a library, but it was not very big. Winston's school had only a few shelves at the back of a classroom; Anne imagined the two or three shelves full of tattered novels which passed for a circulating library at the village post office; Cherry had never even heard of a library. How great, then, was everyone's surprise to be shown into one of the biggest rooms they had ever seen, three of its four walls lined with bookshelves, full of books of all sizes, all ages, and many colours. There was a gasp of awe as they looked at this immense array of knowledge. The fourth wall was mostly taken up with a row of tall windows which looked out across the garden to the paddock, and through which the late afternoon sun was streaming. It made the room warm and drowsy, and filled the air with the smell of old leather bindings.

There was a faded but richly patterned carpet on the floor, two or three tables, some with books and magazines on them, several armchairs, and a big old-fashioned bureau of painted wood with carving and gilt upon it.

Matty got them all to sit round one of the tables. Then she spoke:

'I want to ask you,' she began, 'if you will be kind

enough to help me – that is, as it is the holidays and you may have time to spare. Of course, if any of you are going away immediately, that can't be helped; and if any of you are too busy, you must say so. I'm afraid what I am going to ask you to do may be very dull, but I do hope you won't think it a waste of time.'

She paused, but no one spoke.

'I really do need help rather badly, and I simply don't know who else to ask,' she went on.

Then she stopped again, as if wondering whether she ought to go on.

'Don't you worry, ma'am,' said Winston, 'we'll help if we can, won't we, kids?'

'Oh, yes,' said Anne and Deborah together.

'You'd better wait till I tell you what I want,' said Matty. 'Suppose I begin at the beginning. I expect you will wonder what I am leading up to, but if you listen for a few minutes, you will understand.

'Perhaps you remember that my brother, old Stephen Jay, died last February. I had been looking after him here for many years, and although he was quite old – over seventy – his death was a shock to me. I don't much like being here alone, even with Dennis beside me, and old Dragon out in the paddock; in fact, I'm going to move down to the village in a few days' time. But where was I? Oh yes, I was telling you about my poor brother. I have looked after him for twenty years, ever since his wife died in fact. She died of a disease of the lungs –'

'T.B.?' asked Richard. His father was a doctor, and talked about such things at home pretty often.

'That's right,' answered Matty. 'It's a very terrible thing. My brother and his poor wife had two children; the eldest, a boy, is called Gerald, and he is still alive.

The younger was a girl, and she too died of the same disease as her mother.

'This house, Mulbridge Manor, came to my grandfather over a hundred years ago – about the time Queen Victoria came to the throne. My brother Stephen always told me it should come to me when he died. You may wonder why he did not leave it to his son Gerald. But Gerald – though I hate to say it about my own nephew – is a bad man; it is a pity, if one of them had to die, that it was not he but his sister, who was a sweet girl. However, Gerald is still alive, though I have not seen him for many years. He and my brother quarrelled. It is not so much what he *did* as what he was; I can forgive people many of the things they do, but I can't forgive them hard-heartedness and cruelty and selfishness. Perhaps Gerald had too much money; perhaps my brother spoilt him when he was a boy. But he was always getting into debt through horse-racing and card-playing and sheer extravagance, and he was always coming to his father for money. They quarrelled, and Gerald was terribly rude and cruel in his attitude to his father, even when his father was deeply concerned about his wife's health. He accused Gerald of causing his own mother's death through his ingratitude and his bad ways; I don't think this was true, but it is the kind of thing men say when they get angry. My brother needed help in many ways, but Gerald never did anything for him; he had always hoped that Gerald would take up a profession, be a great lawyer or a doctor or go into Parliament; but Gerald was an idler and waster. In short, he broke his father's heart, and his father refused to pay his debts any longer, or to have anything to do with him.

'During these last ten years or so, my brother has

scarcely been out of the Manor, but has spent his time reading and thinking and studying; he was a learned man and, if he had needed to make money, he could have had a brilliant position in the church or at a university. Instead, he used to write articles for out-of-the-way journals, and – well, he kept very much to himself, and I used to tell him he only lived for his books. "For my books," he would say, "and for my sister, who lives for me. What I should do without my sister Matty, I don't know. I shan't let Gerald have a penny of my money, and he shall certainly not have the house. It will be yours, Matty, when I die – *that* I promise you." "But I don't want the house, Stephen," I told him. "I shan't like it when you are gone. Perhaps I shall go first. Besides, you ought to forgive your son – after all, he is *your* son" – "Don't tell *me* what to do," he would say. "I know my duty. Not another word." For he could be very firm – rude, some people would call it, but I knew better.

'Well, as you know, he died last spring, and when I had time, I began to think about myself. I thought I would move from here and buy a cottage not far away, big enough for myself and Dennis; and I decided I would offer the Manor as a gift to the county, because I knew they would be glad of it for a particular purpose. This county has never been able to afford a proper hospital for diseases of the chest and lungs, and I thought this would be the best possible use for it, seeing that my brother's poor wife and daughter suffered so much in this way. Perhaps if there had been a hospital of this kind in those days, their diseases might have been cured.'

Richard could not help interrupting.

'That's right, Miss Jay,' he said. 'My father says

that what this county needs more than anything is a hospital for chest diseases. He says it's a disgrace, but they haven't much money.'

'You seem to know all about it,' said Matty. 'But let me finish my story. I went to see the County Medical Officer, and of course he said he was delighted, because this is a very good situation for a hospital, as it is quiet and isolated and the air is very good. So he talked to his committee, and they decided to take the house, and I said I wanted no money, but they asked me where I was going to live. In the end, they offered to give me, in exchange for the Manor, enough money to buy myself a cottage, so everything was happily settled – until the awful thing happened.

'A few weeks ago I got a letter from a lawyer in London. It contained a printed notice from a newspaper, which said – Just a moment, I have it here.'

She went quickly across to the painted bureau, opened the top, and took out a long envelope from which she drew a letter and a newspaper cutting.

'This is what the cutting says. "LEGAL NOTICE. Stephen Beverly Jay (deceased). Pursuant to the Trustee Act, 1925 (as amended). Any person having knowledge –"'

Here Matty stopped, noticing that her audience, though listening intently, was beginning to be puzzled.

'But you can't understand it, I'm sure. Nor could I. But reading the letter that came with it, I discovered that my nephew Gerald, whom I had thought to be in Canada, was in England, and was claiming possession of the Manor, as next of kin. That means he was my brother's legal heir, you know, and entitled to claim all his property, unless Stephen had left a will bequeathing it to someone else.

'I went to see this lawyer, which was a foolish thing to do, as it turned out – but I daresay it made no difference. He lives in London, and he is not a pleasant man at all. He as good as told me that I had no right to be living here so long after my brother's death, and that the house belonged to my nephew Gerald. I told him my brother would not have dreamed of leaving it to Gerald, and that he had often told me it was to come to me. As I said before, I didn't want it for myself, but I had already promised it to the County Medical Committee. It was a very awkward situation. The lawyer told me that if my brother had left me the house, he had no doubt put it in his will, and I had better hurry up and produce the will, or my nephew would turn me out and claim the house for himself. I asked what Gerald wanted the house for, and the lawyer said that was nothing to do with me; but I gathered that he meant to sell it for a hotel or a golf-club or something. When I told the lawyer I had promised the house for a hospital, he didn't seem at all interested. He only said it was not mine to promise – that is, unless I could produce my brother's will.'

'So I suppose you did?' said Richard.

'No,' said Matty. 'The fact is, I can't find a will. I have looked everywhere, and there isn't a trace of it. My brother used to keep his private papers in that desk –' she pointed to the painted bureau – 'but when I went through them all, it was nowhere to be found. It wasn't at his bank either. So I went to the solicitor in London with whom my brother used to deal, and he too knew nothing of it. He told me, in fact, that my brother had been a difficult man to deal with; he had been secretive, and of late years had become absent-minded. I knew this myself. But who can blame him, when he had so much disappointment and tragedy in his life? What could I do? Of course I had to go to the County Medical Officer and tell him what had happened. I asked him if he could help me to trace the will, but he only smiled and shook his head. It was the same wherever I went. I could see that nobody believed me. Do *you* believe me?' Matty suddenly asked, looking hard at Richard.

'Yes, Miss Jay,' said Richard promptly, and the others nodded their heads with vigour.

'But no one else does. You see, my dears,' Matty went on, rather sadly, 'I too am getting rather absent-minded. You know, some people in this neighbour-hood – it is a fact, and I am not very proud of it – but *some* people actually call me "Scatty Matty"! You wouldn't believe it, would you?'

All the children looked slightly uncomfortable. It was Winston who saved an awkward situation.

'Of course not,' he said stoutly. 'What on earth should they do that for?'

'Well, you know,' Matty went on apologetically, 'I believe I do do some silly things sometimes, and of course I'm very forgetful. I once went to the police and reported a lost handbag of mine, with eighteen pounds in it, and they searched high and low, and advertised all over the county, and in the end I had to own up that I had found it under my own pillow. So of course nowadays nobody takes me really seriously, and the chairman of the Medical Committee as good as told me I had no business to offer them the Manor as a hospital when it obviously didn't belong to me. He was quite nice about it, but I could see he thought I was barmy.

'But I'm not, you know. Scatty I may be, sometimes, but I'm not barmy. I know that Stephen promised me this house more than once, and even talked about a will. I feel certain there is a will somewhere. Only we shall have to find it quickly. For I'm *not* going to let Gerald have the Manor. My brother would turn in his grave if he thought *that* was going to happen. He meant *me* to have it, and I mean the county to have it for a hospital. I want to show them I was right – and they were wrong not to believe me.'

'Where do you think it might be?' asked Richard, anxious to put aside matters of right and wrong, and be practical.

'It may sound silly, but I feel convinced it's in this room somewhere.'

'But you say you've looked?' said Richard.

'Not everywhere,' said Matty. 'How could I, by myself? But if you'll help me, I'm sure we shall manage it. You know, my brother, as I have said, grew absent-minded – or rather, he got absorbed in his books. I shouldn't be surprised if he left the will in one of these books. It's just the sort of thing he would do, until he had time to take it to the bank or to his lawyer. My brother had quite enough legal knowledge to draw up a will himself, and there were any number of acquaintances he could have got to witness his signature.'

'So you want us to have a look through the books?' said Winston cheerfully. 'That's about it. O.K. When do we start?'

'Oh, do you think you could?' said Matty gratefully. 'That's what I was hoping. I know there are rather a lot –'

'About five to six thousand, I should think,' said Richard, who had been glancing round the shelves.

'But we can have a shot at it. If we do a thousand a day, we can get through them in a week. And if we're lucky, we might find the will the very first day.'

'Splendid,' said Matty. 'That's the spirit. I've looked at a few books, in a casual way, and several of them had papers in them, of one sort and another. Nothing very valuable or interesting, I'm afraid, but it shows that my brother might easily have put his will there and forgotten to take it out.'

'Perhaps he forgot which book he put it in,' said Deborah. '*I* would, with all this lot.'

Suddenly they noticed it was long after six o'clock. It was certainly time to be going home. The sun was still bright, but the shadows were beginning to lengthen. Cherry had almost dropped asleep in her chair. Everyone promised to come next day and begin the search.

'You'd better come early in the afternoon,' said Matty. 'I have to go out myself in the morning – to arrange about my move, you know – but I shall be here at two o'clock, if you can all come; and you can have tea with me after we've made a start.'

'Oh, no,' said Richard. 'We can bring our own tea – can't we, everyone?'

But Matty insisted on their having tea. She had a little help with the house, two or three days a week; Mrs Mead from the village came and gave her a hand, and tomorrow was one of her days.

So it was settled. Only one thing remained to be agreed on.

'You had better not tell anyone what you are doing,' said Matty. 'Let it be a secret between us till we have found what we want. If it gets about that you are looking for a will, there will be a lot of talk, and we don't want that. Tell your parents you are coming up here to help me sort out my brother's library, which is to be sold. That is quite true, you know – you *will* be sorting it out in a way, and afterwards I expect I shall have to sell it. So you won't be telling a lie, and nobody need know what we are really doing until the time comes for telling them. Now you'd all better be going – and thank you for taking a weight off my mind. I didn't know *who* to ask. What luck you came along when you did!'

Then the children said good-bye for the time being, and promised not to be late the following afternoon. Matty saw them out of the door and turned back to discuss things with Dennis. The children set off as fast as they could. It was long past Cherry's bed-time. The Mulcaster four parted from Anne on the heath and left her to hurry home on foot. Anne watched their three bicycles twinkle off in the direction of the road to Mulcaster. Then she turned and started briskly for Mulbridge.

What an adventure! As she went home, she thought of the doctor's words last time he had called on her mother after a bad attack of coughing.

'Now if only we could get you into hospital, Mrs Shipley,' he had said, 'we might do wonders. But there aren't enough beds. They're all full up with cases much worse than yours. Never mind, we must look after you as best we can, and see that it gets no worse.'

But Anne wanted her mother cured. She wanted her never to cough again, never to pass a sleepless night with pains in her chest. So now she pictured her in one of the rooms on the sunny side of the Manor, being looked after by white-aproned nurses and given just the treatment she needed.

'It's got to be found,' she said to herself. 'It's got to be found. Then there'll be the hospital for Mummy, just near home. Between us, we've got to find that will.'

Then she suddenly thought of her mother in bed, perhaps wondering when Anne would get home. She quickened her pace as she reached Mulbridge Woods and began to run.

Chapter Four

THE SEARCH BEGINS

NEXT day the sun shone bright and hot once more. Richard and Cherry finished lunch in good time and were again cycling along the road to the heath. Richard had made Cherry swear to say nothing to anybody about a will. It was he who made the explanation to their parents, and answered their questions. But there was no difficulty in getting away. Miss Jay, though scatty, was well-known to be harmless and respectable; Mrs Masters had no objection to her children doing anything so useful as helping the old lady sort out her library.

'What is a "will", Richard?' Cherry asked, from the carrier of Richard's creaking bicycle.

'A will,' answered her brother, 'is something saying who you leave your property to when you die. Your property means your house and money and that sort of thing.'

'But what is a will like?' persisted Cherry.

'It's a sheet of paper with writing on it.'

'Have you ever seen one?'

'No, I haven't.'

'Well, how do you know what it's like?'

'I just *know*,' said Richard with finality.

'But how shall *I* know if I find it?' asked Cherry.

'I don't suppose you'll find it.'

'I might. I bet I will.'

'Well, if you find anything you think might be a will – in fact, if you find any papers with writing on them, you can bring them to me. Now don't ask any more questions. We're coming to the steep bit, and I don't want to talk any more.'

The Jones children were waiting outside their gate. All four went on towards the Manor together. They found Anne already there, eager to begin the search. But she had not dared go in alone.

They wheeled their cycles into the drive and presented themselves at the front door. Once more the rusty bell jangled far off in the house, and once more Dennis's sonorous bark was heard signalling their arrival.

Matty was in a cheerful mood.

'Now, isn't that nice!' she said. 'It's jolly good of you all to come up. You know, I've a feeling one of you is *bound* to find the will. *Then* how pleased we shall all be.'

'And *I've* a feeling,' piped Cherry, 'that it's going to be *me*.'

First, Matty insisted on showing them over the great rambling Manor. They had seen the dining-room and the library, so she led the way along a wide, flagged passage to the kitchen premises. Mrs Mead from the village was in the kitchen pottering about, doing various odd jobs. She greeted them with:

'My, what a lark! Fancy you all comin' here to help Miss Jay with them books. You've got a job in front of you, you haven't half.'

The children looked at the great chimney-piece, where the huge roasts had been cooked in the old days; the deep cupboards now nearly as empty as Mother Hubbard's; the spacious dairy where the milk, butter, and eggs from the home farm had been kept. But now there was no home farm, and the great stone slabs and meat-safes were empty.

They followed Matty up the broad oak staircase with its panelled walls and turned wooden balustrade. Room after room was opened to them; there were pictures on the walls, heavy dark portraits of ladies and gentlemen of bygone days; faded brocade curtains and worn carpets; old cupboards and bedsteads; linen-presses, and dim, spotted mirrors in gilt frames.

'Much too big for Stephen and me, of course,' said Matty. 'It will be a good thing if it's put to a better use. Think of all these old plaster walls painted a nice cheerful white, or cream, and nice bright lights everywhere, and new curtains. It's just the place for a quiet, restful home for sick people. Look at the views too.'

They went over to the window; they were in a room on the south side overlooking the garden, the paddock, and the heath. The sun was streaming in. Beyond the heath they could see the old grey church tower at Mulbridge, the elm trees, and the distant fields rolling away towards Mulcaster.

'On a clear day,' said Matty, 'you can see the cathedral quite clearly. Too much haze just now, though.'

Anne was imagining her mother in just such a room as this, propped against pillows in a neat, white bed, and looking out of the sunny window towards the roofs of Mulcaster and the distant sea. Back in their cottage, Anne had left her mother, sitting in the rocking-chair, which she had carried out into the sunshine; the invalid was better today, but Anne had made her promise not to overwork, for it was overwork that brought on her fits of coughing.

They were shown the bedroom that old Mr Jay had occupied. Richard looked round it carefully, wondering whether perhaps the will was concealed somewhere in this very room. But Matty assured him that it had been thoroughly searched. If the will was to be found, it was in that huge library below – the room where the old man had spent most of his time.

Back to the library they went. Mrs Mead came in to ask Matty something about the household arrangements.

'All right,' she said. 'I'll come at once. Now, my dears, I must leave you to begin looking. I think, Richard, you had better be in charge. Look anywhere you like, and go anywhere you like; and if you want to ask me any questions, come and find me. I've got a lot of turning out to do, for as you know, I'm moving down to the village at the end of the week. Don't go and overwork and get fed up, will you? When you want a change, just go into the garden or the paddock. I'm sure you can find your way to the orchard if you want any plums. I believe you may find some of the little red apples ripe enough to eat too. But mind – don't give yourself collywobbles, whatever you do! That would never do – would it, Dennis? Now where did I put my spectacles? Bless me, I know I had them. Well, perhaps they're in the kitchen.'

And so saying, off she rambled, followed by the old half-blind retriever. The children were left to themselves.

'Now,' said Richard, 'first let's gather round this table and decide on a plan of campaign.'

'When are we going to find the will?' asked the irrepressible Cherry. 'Hadn't we better do that first?'

Cherry was told to shut up.

'I say,' said Anne, 'what a smashing house! I wonder if there's a secret passage.'

'Sure to be,' agreed Deborah. 'Let's ask Matty.'

'Cut it out, girls,' said Winston sternly. 'We're not here for our health. We've got a job to do.'

'Order, order!' said Richard. 'I vote we make this table our centre. Any of you who find any papers, lay them on the table. If they look like being a will, better tell me. Take all papers out of books – that is, loose papers, not just odd pages. You'd better start in that corner, Cherry. Only do the books in the bottom shelf. And for heaven's sake, don't miss any out, or we shall never know which have been done and which haven't. Anne, you'd better take the second shelf up, starting over there. Deborah, will you start on the third shelf? Put every book back when you've finished with it. Don't miss any out. Winston, you take the fourth shelf.'

'O.K.,' said Winston. 'What about all those magazines?'

He pointed to a long row of unbound journals near the end of the fourth shelf.

'Better go through them,' said Richard. 'Can't afford to miss *anything*.'

'What are *you* going to do, Richard?' asked Cherry.

'I shall use those steps and start on the fifth shelf up,' answered Richard.

A set of mahogany library steps stood in one corner of the room, with an upright pole at one side to steady yourself with, and a little platform at the top to rest the books on while you were turning the pages.

'Oh, can't I use the steps?' asked Cherry eagerly.

'No,' said Richard. 'You'd fall and break your neck. That wouldn't help.'

Cherry protested, but in a minute or two she agreed to do as her hero brother ordered; so, squatting on the floor, she began to pull the books out of the bottom shelf, one by one, and patiently turn the pages.

Anne had already made a start on the second shelf. Deborah, for once quite practical, began on shelf number three, and Winston on the shelf above. For a few minutes nothing was to be heard except the dull thud of books being laid on the floor or on a table, and the flipping of pages as they were turned by the hands of the searchers.

'I've found it!' said Cherry at last, in great excitement. 'I've found the will, Richard.'

'Where?' cried Anne. 'Show me, Cherry!'

Richard descended from the steps and took the small sheet of poor quality paper that his sister handed him. '"Babbage and Son, Booksellers, Exeter",' he read. '"Forsyth: History of the Japanese People, 3 vols. 27s. Post, 1s. 10d." This is nothing but a bill!' he concluded, tossing the piece of paper on to the table.

Cherry was not discouraged.

'Anyway,' she said, 'I *nearly* found it. A bill *is* nearly a will, isn't it?'

'Don't call me every time you find a will,' said Richard, 'but just put them on the centre table, there's a good Cherry Blossom. I expect every book you look at is bursting with hidden documents.'

They went on with the search. After half an hour they had found three or four old papers, part of a map, another couple of bills, and a folder advertising a new fodder for horses.

'I say,' said Deborah, 'look at this funny old book, Anne! It's full of pictures of South Sea islanders and animals and things, and the women are all in funny skirts and the men have painted faces.'

Anne and Deborah were soon lost in a Victorian

47

picture-book. Richard realized that the search was
going to be a long business. Between them they had
scarcely searched a hundred books before the first
hour had passed. He began to work out in his mind
one of those problems his mathematics master used
to set for prep. 'If four children take one hour to
search a hundred books, how many days will it take
them, searching for four hours a day, to deal with five
thousand books? The answer should be given to the
nearest minute.'

Then Mrs Mead looked in to see what they were at.
She distracted Cherry by talking to her, disturbed
everyone, and got in the way.

'Hadn't I better come around with my duster?' she
said. 'My, what a mess you're getting in! I've never
seen so much dust in all my life.'

But Richard tactfully persuaded her to be gone, and
continued his methodical investigations into the books
on the fifth, sixth, and seventh shelves.

'Wonder if the old geyser *read* all this stuff,' said
Winston. 'Look what I've got here. "Sermons of the
Rev. Thomas Critch-ton" in five volumes. Vol. I,
Vol. II, Vol. III –'

'That's pronounced "Cry-ton",' said Richard, 'not
"Critchton", and you needn't *read* all the books – you
only have to find the missing will. And if you ask me,
that's going to take all our time.'

'You're telling me,' agreed Winston, returning to
the pursuit.

Once more Mrs Mead interrupted. This time she
wanted to know if anyone had a watch; she was to get
tea at five, she said, and she had no idea of the time.
Richard told her. Once more she pottered off to the
kitchen.

'We'll never get anywhere at this rate,' thought Richard, but he did not say so. It would not do for the organizer to show he was discouraged. Another hour's search had produced some more letters, some playing-cards, and whist-drive tickets, which had evidently been used as book-markers, some more bills, a few circulars, and a picture-postcard of Ramsgate as it might have been fifty years ago, with long-skirted, tightly-belted ladies in straw hats sunning themselves by the shore. The girls were getting bored. Long sighs escaped from Deborah; she took a pile of books to the painted bureau, but instead of looking through the pages, she allowed herself to dream over the quaint carvings and designs on its surface. Cherry had given up the search and longed to be out in the sunshine. Even Anne was getting weary. Winston went doggedly on through the five volumes of the Rev. Crichton's Sermons, seven volumes of the Rev. Alexander Carmichael's Discourses, a great number of leather-bound theological works, and the fifty or sixty unbound journals of some antiquarian society.

'Talk about a perishing needle in a so-and-so haystack,' he muttered to himself at intervals.

At last Matty herself looked in with the welcome news that tea was ready.

'Suppose you all come into the kitchen and wash your hands,' she suggested. 'You must be up to your eyes in dust! Then we'll see what Mrs Mead has got us for tea, shall we?'

Mrs Mead, inveterate potterer though she was, had prepared a wonderful tea, and it looked, too, as if Matty had remembered to visit the pastrycook's in the morning. There were little square sandwiches, some of fish-paste and some of water-cress, doughnuts, macaroons, jam tarts, orangeade, and as many ripe Victoria plums as anyone had room for. They sat down this time, not in the low dark dining-room, but in the big square kitchen, with its scrubbed deal table, and shining, varnished dresser.

Matty had a little pot of tea to herself. As the children's strength began to revive with the effects of Mrs Mead's sandwiches, and the cakes and orangeade, they chattered and laughed and asked their hostess a hundred questions.

'Is there a ghost of the Manor?' asked Deborah.

'Oh, yes,' said Matty. 'I should jolly well think so. But I must say, I've never seen it, and I don't know anyone who has.'

'And is there a secret passage?' asked Anne.

'Yes, indeed. Behind one of the panels in the dining-room there's a priest's hole, as they call them. You see, in the old days Roman Catholic priests had to hide, and sometimes the great houses had secret hiding-places to shelter priests from the Puritan magistrates. I'm afraid ours isn't much of a place though – just a tiny bare room up a little narrow flight of stone steps.'

She promised to show it later.

When tea was over, Anne said she must go. She was getting anxious about her mother. Mrs Robins had promised to look in, but Anne felt that she must go home herself and see that she wasn't doing too much. If Anne knew her mother, she would probably be turning out the larder or hoeing the runner-bean rows.

Anne set off for home after promising to come at the same time next day. Cherry and Deborah helped Mrs Mead clear away and wash up the tea-things. Richard led Winston off into the library to have a council of war.

'I tell you what,' he said, 'we can't all go on all the time like this. Deborah and Cherry mess about half the time, and that woman – what's her name? Mrs Mead – keeps on butting in and stopping us working.'

'What we need,' said Winston, 'is a plan – I mean, a timetable. So many hours on duty, so many hours' leave. See?'

'What we need,' said Richard, 'is a headquarters – not this library, but somewhere *outside*, where we shan't be disturbed.'

'Good idea,' said Winston.

'Then we can work out a real plan, and talk about things a bit. I don't believe the old boy just shoved his will into some book – one of about five thousand: he can't have been quite so absent-minded. We must question Matty and see if she can give us a clue.'

By now it was time they were all getting home. It was agreed between the two boys that tomorrow they would consider the question of having a headquarters somewhere in the grounds, and the girls could be given the job of getting it ready. That would be a change from going through books.

They found their two sisters in the dining-room peering through an open panel, while Matty further explained the use of a priest's hole.

'Spooky, isn't it?' said Cherry. 'I don't like it. Let's come away.'

'It's terribly romantic,' said Deborah. 'Fancy some poor priest shivering in there while troopers were searching the house for him!'

The boys examined the hiding-place, but there was little to be seen there.

'Come on, kids,' said Winston, 'better beat it now. They'll be wondering what's happened to us.'

So they thanked Matty for their tea, agreed to come the next day, bringing their own food, said good-bye, and made for home.

One thing was evident. They had taken on no small job. Perhaps the will would turn up in the very next book they opened; but Richard had a feeling that they were only at the beginning of the problem.

Chapter Five

HEADQUARTERS

NEXT afternoon Richard brought along a school friend of his called Beaver. His real name was something quite different, but nobody ever used it. Perhaps it was his prominent teeth, with which he doggedly chewed pencils in class, that had earned him the nickname; perhaps it was his quiet, persistent manner of working. Although nearly thirteen, and several months older than Richard, and although half a head taller, he admired Richard as one of Napoleon's marshals might have worshipped his Emperor. Very brainy, he thought Richard, very brainy indeed; more brainy than anyone else of his age at school. So he would do anything Richard asked. He had very little use for books. His head was as full of aeroplanes and engine-numbers as his pockets were full of marbles, pencil-sharpeners, pen-knives, and other really important possessions.

Richard had simply asked him to come and help with Miss Jay's library. He had not told him about

the will, for Matty had forbidden this. He introduced
Beaver to Matty.

'This is my friend, Beaver,' he said. 'He has come
to help. We can do with all the help we can get, and
Beaver was at a loose end. He's absolutely reliable, Miss
Jay. I give you my word.'

Then he drew the surprised Matty to the far end of
the library and, speaking as loudly as he dared, added:
'In the circumstances, may I tell him what we are
looking for? I assure you, it will go no further.'

'But of course,' agreed Matty. 'You say he is
reliable, and that's enough for us – isn't it, Dennis?'

Dennis said he wasn't sure, but as Miss Jay had
given her permission, Richard felt he could explain the
situation to his friend.

'It's like this, Beaver,' he said. 'We're not really
arranging the books, we're looking through them for
an important document.'

'Five pound note or something?' Beaver guessed.

'Something much more valuable. A will. When Miss
Jay's brother died, he left his will hidden somewhere
in this library. We're searching all the books.'

Beaver nodded. That was enough for him. The
sooner they got on with it, the better.

There was something else that had to be arranged.

'Miss Jay,' said Richard, 'we thought it might be
a good idea if we could have our own Headquarters –
somewhere outside, one of the sheds perhaps. Then
we needn't be disturbed; we could have our food there
on wet days; we thought it would be a good idea, if
you don't object.'

'But of course not,' said Matty. 'Let me see – what
about the potting-shed? No, wouldn't do. Too many
spiders. I have it. Just the place. Follow me.'

Richard and the two boys, together with Deborah and Anne, with Cherry and the black retriever bringing up the rear, followed Miss Jay out through the french windows into the garden. She led them first down a flagged path, then down a gravel path, until they came to the edge of the paddock. She pushed open the door of an old, wooden barn and told them to look inside. It was a big building, ancient and lofty, with a tiled roof and many twisted beams.

'There,' she said, 'what about that? Nobody ever comes here. You can do what you like, but you'd better not have a fire. Don't suppose you'll want one this weather, anyway. Jolly good place, if you ask me. Bit musty, I dare say, and the roof's leaky in wet weather, but only at the far end. I expect you'll make it all ship-shape in no time.'

She was greeted with cries of delight and admiration. It was just the place.

'I must get back to my packing,' said Matty suddenly. 'The trouble is, if I stop, I forget what I've packed; then I have to unpack everything to find out. So long, dears. We'll see you later. Come along, Dennis.'

Before they could thank her, she was off down the gravel path towards the house.

The children made a rapid tour of the interior of their new Headquarters. Then they sat down on some piles of straw and had a brief council meeting.

'Look here,' began Richard, 'I vote we split up – some of us go on looking through the books, and the others prepare Headquarters and get food ready.'

'That's right,' agreed Winston. 'Divide forces. Obvious thing to do.'

Beaver nodded vigorously.

'Obvious,' he said.

'You'd better work in the library, Richard,' said Anne.

'That's right,' said Winston. 'Richard knows about wills and things.'

Again Beaver nodded.

'Very clever chap, Richard,' he confirmed.

'I'll arrange Headquarters,' said Deborah. 'Cherry can help me.'

'Oh, no, I want to find the will,' Cherry protested.

'You can find it later,' said Richard. 'You help Deborah for today.'

Anne was torn. There was nothing she loved better than making a home in a shed or barn, but she longed to find the will, for her mother's sake.

'What shall I do, Richard?' she asked.

'Tell you what,' suggested Winston. 'Me and Richard and Beaver can start on the books, and you girls get the H.Q. ready. How's that?'

So it was decided. But first, they all went to the drive gates to bring their cycles in. From now on, they should be kept in the barn. Then they would be safe, and ready to hand if wanted in a hurry.

At last, leaving the girls to organize H.Q., Richard and his two lieutenants returned to the library to recommence the search.

Outside, the sun shone as if it would never stop; the untidy garden slept, its flower-scented slumber scarcely disturbed by the drone of bees and the drowsy twitter of birds; beyond it, the paddock lay in a haze of heat; the old horse, Dragon, stood under the shade of a tree hardly bothering to crop the long grass at his feet.

A boy of very few words, Beaver settled down with

a new piece of chewing-gum in his cheek and a huge pile of dusty volumes in front of him. His orders were simple: all loose papers to be taken out and placed on the centre table; then the books were to be put back in their shelves. Even Beaver could scarcely go wrong.

Winston took a turn at the library steps, pulling out volumes from the higher shelves and extracting all loose papers, however unimportant they seemed. Richard settled down at the centre table to write a journal of their proceedings. He had brought with him for the purpose a new exercise-book. Opening it at the first page, he wrote:

'Operation W. Log-book. Private.'

On the second page he wrote:

'First Day: Wednesday, 3 August. Mission begins. R.M., W.J., D.J., A.S., and C.M. assigned mission to discover W. Refreshments provided by M.J.

'Second Day: Thursday, 4 August. Operation commenced. No results so far. Tea provided by M.J.

'Third Day: Friday, 5 August. H.Q. set up in paddock barn, by kind permission of M.J. Party joined by B. Search continues.'

After that, there was nothing more to be written. Richard closed the book and started once more turning the leaves of the late Stephen Jay's innumerable volumes. As he did so, he felt that this was a very hit-or-miss method. They might go on for weeks at this rate. He wondered how much time they had. How soon would Matty's wicked nephew send down some policeman or perhaps troops to turn them out and seize the Manor for himself? At any rate, he must have a talk with Miss Jay. Opening the private journal once more at the second page, he wrote:

'Memo. Must consult M.J. and see whether she can suggest any clues to work on. What were S.J.'s favourite books, etc.?'

The English master was always telling him not to use the expression 'etc.', but it was a jolly useful word when you weren't sure what to put next.

Time wore on. Once again, old letters, bills, lists of one sort and another were found, but nothing resembling a will. At least Richard was surer now of what they were looking for than he had been the day before. Yesterday evening, in conversation with his father he had craftily led the talk round to the subject of wills. He had pretended – without actually saying as much – that the matter had arisen out of a book he was reading at the time.

'By the way, Daddy,' he began, 'have you ever seen a person's will? What does it look like?'

'Yes, I've seen a will,' said Dr Masters. 'There's nothing very special about it. Just a printed form with a lot of lawyer's nonsense on it.'

'Anything like a doctor's prescription?' asked Richard.

'Heavens, no!' said his father with a laugh. 'No one has to read my prescriptions except a chemist, and chemists are used to them. A will has to be read by all sorts of people, so for one thing it's usually typewritten, or at least written out in decent handwriting.'

'What does it say on the outside?' persisted Richard.

'Blowed if I know,' answered Dr Masters. 'The last one I saw just said "Will of So-and-so Esquire", I think. What do you want to know for?'

But Richard was ready for this.

'Oh, I was having an argument with another boy about it the other day. There was something about it in a book. Are wills made of parchment or sheepskin or something like that?'

'Not nowadays. Too expensive. Nowadays they're on ordinary paper, often a printed form. You'd probably find the words "Last Will and Testament of W. W. Snooks" or whoever it is. But I say, if you keep me talking here any longer, I shall be late for surgery.'

This suited Richard well. He did not want his father asking any more questions; he had learnt just what he wanted to know. 'Last Will and Testament' – that was the thing to look out for. Well, he would see to it that no 'last will and testament' escaped his eye.

Meanwhile, the girls had been busy making headquarters presentable and ship-shape, as Miss Jay called it. They made a rough council table from two old trestles which they dragged out from under the straw, and some cracked elm boards which stood against the wall. Seats were a problem, but Matty gave them permission to collect four old packing-cases from the potting-shed and the dairy.

Cherry built the straw into a kind of sofa at the far end of the barn, for anyone to have a rest on who was tired of searching old books. Some disused potato sacks from the potting shed were hung up as curtains.

There was something of an argument about flowers.

'They'll only laugh at us if we have flowers,' said Deborah.

'Let them,' said Anne. 'I'm going to have flowers. A home isn't a home without flowers – that's what Mummy says.'

'This isn't a home,' objected Deborah, 'it's a head-quarters.'

'Why shouldn't a headquarters be a home?' asked Anne.

She got her way.

Cherry was sent to the kitchen for a jam-pot, and Anne went round the garden picking a few flowers here and a few there, not taking too many of any one kind. The flowers were placed in the centre of the council table.

A window-sill was brushed clean of dust, cobwebs, and dead flies; lined with clean newspaper, it served as a shelf.

Next there was the problem of the cupboard 'for spare food, stores, and etcetera', as Anne expressed it. The best they could find was an old trunk from the tool-shed. They cleaned it out, lined it with news-paper, and placed it in a corner beside the sofa of straw.

In spite of the spiders' webs and empty birds' nests high up in the rafters and quite out of reach, and in spite of all the litter and rubbish which they did their best to tidy up, the barn began to look quite habitable. Perhaps the most exciting and picturesque feature was an old pony trap resting on its shafts at one end of the barn. Cherry climbed into it with a cry of joy and sat on one of the two seats fixed against its sides.

'This can be the dining-room,' she said. 'Oh, Deborah, let's have tea here. Look, it's lovely!'

This was certainly an idea. Both the others were impressed with Cherry's suggestion. The trouble was, for this purpose it was decidedly sloping. The problem was to make it level, otherwise food and drink were going to go rolling and spilling all over the dining-room. Between them they managed to raise the trap by its shafts and drag it to the wall, where a beam at a convenient height made it possible for them to rest the ends of the shafts on it, and so make the floor just about horizontal. The difficulty was, the whole thing might slip when somebody climbed in. Some old but still sound rope was discovered, and with this they tied the ends of the shafts to the beam on which they rested. For additional safety they found two bricks and wedged them in against the wheels, on the floor of the barn.

'There,' said Anne, 'it won't run away now, even when Beaver climbs in.'

The next thing was to get tea ready. Matty lent them a big tin tray and some plates and cups from the kitchen. Anne promised to bring a table-cloth from home, as they did not like to ask Matty for too much. The driver's seat in the pony-trap was used as a table, and on this were spread out the sandwiches, buns, fruit, and bottles of fizz. Soon all was ready, and while Deborah and Anne put the finishing touches to everything, Cherry was sent to the library to fetch the boys.

'Hullo, Richard,' she said. 'Found the will yet? Well, anyway, we've made a smashing headquarters. Come and see. Tea's ready.'

The news was welcome. All three boys knocked off without delay and went to wash their hands in the kitchen. Few things are dustier than a neglected library. Then they joined the girls in the paddock barn.

'Not bad,' said Winston. 'Eh, Beaver?'

Beaver nodded appreciatively.

Nothing was said about the flowers on the council table. It was taken for granted that if girls were in

charge, there would be flowers and curtains and that
sort of thing.

It was discovered that the seats in the pony trap
were hinged lids covering empty lockers or compart-
ments, and it was decided to use these for food and
crockery and keep other things in the trunk under the

table. Into this Richard put the private log-book,
which he proposed to read to the company after tea.

Meanwhile, there was food and drink to be con-
sumed: everyone climbed into the two-wheeled dining-
room, and soon there was nothing to be heard but the
popping of bottles and munching of buns and biscuits.
From these high seats they could see out through the
open door across the paddock towards the red brick
wall bounding the Manor grounds. Beyond that lay the

heath and the distant tops of Mulbridge Woods. None of them had ever known a more delightful dining-room. It was too hot to say much, too hot even to eat very energetically. Leisurely mouthfuls were interrupted only by long sighs of contentment.

Chapter Six

'UNDER THE GREEN TREE'

NOTHING was done during the week-end. All the children enjoyed the continued fine weather by going with their parents down to the sea – all, that is, except Anne. Mr Shipley returned from Portsmouth on Saturday afternoon, but he had to go back for at least another week on Monday. Mrs Shipley was still far from well, so Anne stayed at home and managed things for both her parents. She made her mother stay in bed for breakfast, though the invalid insisted on getting up during the morning. Still, she was not strong enough to do everything herself. She had to rest as much as she could.

On Monday morning, when Mr Shipley went off once more to Portsmouth, Anne cleaned the house and went out to do the shopping, while her mother washed. Anne would have done the washing too, but her mother would not let her.

'I can manage nicely, dear,' she said, 'if I just go along at my own pace. And if you do the shopping for me, I shall have plenty of time. After dinner you must go out and play. I can't have you stopping at home every day on my account.'

When Anne got back from the village, she found Deborah Jones waiting for her.

'Can you come?' asked Deborah. 'We're all going up to the Manor again after dinner. *You* know why,' she added in a significant whisper in case Mrs Shipley should overhear.

'Yes, I know,' said Anne, 'but I don't think I'd better come. I want to very badly, but you know what Mondays are. I don't think I ought to leave Mummy. I'll come tomorrow if I can.'

This was very good of Anne, because her mother had already said she might go and play after dinner; but the sight of her mother's tired, strained face worried Anne, and she made up her mind to stay. Perhaps she would go along for an hour after tea, but she wasn't going to promise. All the same, she would have dearly loved to help search for the will, and be with her friends in the paddock barn.

Deborah went off reluctantly to join the others.

'I say, Richard,' said Deborah that afternoon, when they had parked their cycles safely at headquarters, 'I think we ought to have a council meeting.'

Richard was surprised that Deborah should have anything so practical to suggest.

'All right,' he said, 'let's have one now.'

He sat at the council table on an upturned packing-case, with the private journal in front of him. The others sat on the straw sofa.

'What's it all about?' he asked Deborah.

'Well,' began Deborah, 'it's about Anne.'

'Isn't she coming?' asked someone.

'No,' Deborah went on, 'her mother's not very well yet, and Anne's staying in to help. I think it would be a good idea if *we* could help in some way.'

'How?' asked Winston.

'Can't we go and do some of the housework and the shopping and things, so that Anne could come up here?'

'Quite right,' agreed Richard, and Beaver nodded approvingly.

'Hear, hear!' said Winston. 'Doesn't seem right she can't be here. She's in on it, and she oughtn't to be stuck at home all the time.'

'I propose,' said Richard, 'that we go down to the village in turn and help Anne's mother. What about it?'

'Hear, hear!' said two or three voices.

'Good idea,' said Cherry. 'I'd love to help Anne. I can make beds and sweep and all sorts of things. Can't I, Richard?'

'Do we all agree?' asked Richard, ignoring his sister's question.

Everyone agreed.

'Any against?' said Richard.

No one spoke.

'Right. Then we'll draw up a rota.'

This sounded very grand; Beaver supported the

66

suggestion vigorously, having no idea what it meant, but trusting Richard instinctively.

'You draw it up,' said Beaver.

'Everyone agreed?' asked Richard.

'Shall we go in pairs or singly?' asked Winston.

'What do you think?'

There was some argument over this point. In the end it was agreed that they should go in pairs to help Mrs Shipley for as long as she needed – Richard and Deborah in the morning (with Cherry thrown in as an extra), and Winston and Beaver in the afternoon. Beaver would have preferred to assist the leader but he was an obliging boy.

Half an hour later Anne and her mother were surprised by the appearance at the cottage door of Winston and Beaver, who were both rather cleaner and tidier than usual.

'Afternoon, m'm,' began Winston. 'We've been detailed to come down and help, so that Anne can be at the Manor.'

'That's very kind of you,' said Mrs Shipley, 'but do we really need help, sweetheart?'

'Oh, yes, Mummy, let them help if they want to.'

'Orders,' explained Winston briefly. 'Me and Beaver are coming in the afternoons and the others in the morning. We'll do anything you want. I can make pastry if you like – but I'm better at scrubbing floors.'

So Mrs Shipley agreed to accept their help, while Anne went off on her cycle towards the Manor.

Meanwhile, as soon as the council meeting had broken up, Richard, Cherry, and Deborah made their way towards the library to resume the search. When they stepped out of the shady barn into the bright sunshine, they were surprised to see a man standing in the middle of the paddock apparently gazing at Dragon, the old horse.

'Seedy-looking individual,' said Richard, who had read this expression somewhere in a book.

The children gazed for a few moments at the man. He was of medium height, thin, and stringy, and wore an old sports jacket, somewhat out at elbow, and grey flannel trousers. He had a squashed trilby hat on his

head, and round his neck was a dirty grey muffler of artificial silk. Having finished his scrutiny of Dragon he strolled casually across to where the children were standing. They stared back at him, wondering whether he was a friend of Matty's, but thinking he could hardly be this.

'Hullo, young fellow,' said the seedy individual in most friendly tones, 'you'll know me next time, won't you?'

Richard said nothing, but his sister piped up:

'Are you a friend of Sc— I mean, Miss Jay's? She's very particular.'

'I know the lady all right,' said the seedy man casually. 'Nice old horse she's got there. Know if she wants to sell him?'

'I don't know,' said Deborah. 'Do you buy horses?'

'I wouldn't mind thinking about *that* one.'

'Have you spoken to Miss Jay about it?' asked Richard. For all he knew, she might be wanting to sell the horse. After all, she was moving, and she could hardly take Dragon with her.

'Haven't said anything yet,' said the man. 'Nice place she's got here. Do you live with her?'

'Oh, no,' said Cherry, 'we're just helping –'

'We're friends of Miss Jay,' Richard interrupted. 'If you want to speak to her, I expect she's in now.'

'Don't think I'll trouble her just now,' said the man. 'Nice for you kids to have a place like this to come to. Expect there's plenty for you to do here, eh?'

'Oh, yes,' Cherry began, but this time Deborah broke in.

'I hope you're not trespassing,' she said boldly. 'I mean –'

'Lor' bless you, no,' said the man, laughing. 'Now what should I do trespassing in a nice sort of place like this? I often step round here of an afternoon. But I'll be getting along. Got business to do. Tell Miss – er – Jay, if you see her, that there's someone would be interested in buying the old horse if she wants to sell, will you?'

'Who shall we say inquired?' asked Richard, who sometimes took messages over the doctor's telephone.

'Oh, just say – er – well, never mind that. You find out if she's willing to sell. I'll be about here again some time, and then you can tell me what she says.

Here, kiddy,' he said, speaking to Cherry, 'you like
sweets, I'm sure. Try these – catch.'

He pulled a bag of sweets from his pocket and tossed
them towards Cherry. She picked them up and was
about to thank the stranger, but he had already begun
strolling away towards the gates. In a few moments
he disappeared out of the Manor grounds, and they
saw him sauntering across the heath towards Mulcaster.

'You're not to take the sweets, Cherry,' said
Richard. 'You know what Daddy said.'

'They're in papers,' said Cherry. 'I shan't get
germs.'

'Never mind,' said her brother firmly. 'Don't take
sweets from people you don't know. Give them to
me.'

He stuffed the bag in his pocket, determined to
throw it away at the first opportunity. He profoundly
mistrusted presents from total strangers. In books they
were always drugged or poisoned. Not that the seedy
stranger looked that sort of man, but you never knew.

'Wonder why he wanted old Dragon,' said Richard.

'I don't think he did,' said Deborah.

'Why not?'

'I don't know. I just don't *think* he really wants a
horse.'

'Then what do you suppose he was here for?'

'Don't know.'

'Just some tramp, I expect. There's a lot of funny
people on the heath at times – gipsies and such like.'

'"*My* mother said,"' began Deborah, '"*I* never
should –"'

'Come on,' urged Richard. 'We'll never get through
those books. It's nearly three already.'

Back in the library once more, they began methodically going through piles of old volumes, extracting letters and book-markers and odd scraps of paper, but never finding the precious document they were after.

'Look here,' said Richard at last. 'We'll get nowhere like this. Do you mind taking charge for a bit, Deborah?'

'All right,' agreed Deborah. 'Don't be too long.'

'Can I come with you, Richard?' pleaded Cherry.

'No,' said Richard. 'You stay and help Deborah. I won't be long. And if old Seedy turns up, come and find Miss Jay and me.'

Richard had decided he must have a talk with Matty. He found her in a sort of housekeeper's room next to the kitchen, which she used a good deal. The room was in the utmost disorder. Suitcases and hat-boxes, half packed, stood everywhere. Piles of papers and clothes occupied most of the chairs. A quarter pound packet of tea, a ball of string, some clothes-hangers, and a pot of jam jostled one another on the sideboard. In the midst of it all stood Matty, cheerfully humming to herself, while Dennis lay curled up on the hearth-rug.

'Miss Jay,' said Richard. 'I wonder if I could speak to you?'

'Of course, of course,' said Matty. 'Hand me that packet of labels, will you. Thank you. It's a terrible business, moving, you know. I was to have gone last Friday, but I just wasn't ready. I'm off tomorrow, though. I shan't be far away, you know. You can go on coming here – that is, if you're not tired of looking. You haven't come to tell me you've found the will, I suppose?'

'I'm afraid not. In fact, I want to ask you some questions. Are you terribly busy?'

'As you see,' said Matty, waving her hand over the muddle, 'but I can certainly talk to you, Richard. How are you getting on?'

Richard explained briefly what they had done so far. He told her about headquarters, about the plan to help Anne's mother, and about Seedy and his interest in Dragon.

'But I don't want to sell Dragon!' said Matty. 'What on earth should I do that for? Who is the man? He doesn't sound like anybody I know. But I'm afraid some funny people wander round here sometimes, and I don't remember them all. People say I'm a bit funny myself, don't they, Dennis? Perhaps I am. But I certainly shan't part with Dragon. He'll stay in the paddock, whether I'm here or not.'

'Miss Jay,' said Richard, returning to the subject of the search, 'I wonder if you can tell us anything which might help. I mean, for instance, what were Mr Jay's favourite books? You see, there are so many, and I wondered if –'

'Yes, yes, to be sure. I had thought of that. Of course he was always fond of Shakespeare, and – let me see, yes, Dickens. Then he was always consulting dictionaries and legal books and encyclopedias and dry things like that. He was interested in so many subjects, you know. And novels – I mean modern novels, too, not trash but really good ones by all the best writers. You know, he might have left his will in almost any book in the library. That's the trouble.'

'You're sure you can't suggest which?'

'Oh, no. But he was positive about there being a will. He grew dreadfully absent-minded in the last few years; what's more, he wouldn't trust other people with his affairs. It makes it all very difficult.'

'You don't think he could have – well, just lost the will somewhere? I mean, when he was out perhaps.'

'No, I don't think so. Although he was so absent-minded and secretive, he was quite methodical. Not like me. I do things any old how. Stephen used to pull my leg about it. "You're such an old muddler, Matt," he used to say – he often called me Matt, particularly when he was teasing me – "you're such an old muddler that you can't be trusted to do anything properly. All the same, you shall have the Manor when I die. Trust me. Gerald shall never get it, even though he expects it. I'll see to that." That's what he used to say.'

'When was the last time he mentioned his will?' asked Richard.

'Well, now, let me see. You know, I can't remember. It used to upset me so much when he talked of dying, that I probably didn't pay much attention. Then for some days before he died, he was very ill, you know, and wandered in his mind, as old people do. Let me think –'

'Did he say *anything* that might give us a clue?'

Matty pondered for some time. Then she said:

'Well, there was one thing he kept saying, but I couldn't make head or tail of it. It was – let me think of the exact words – I *think* it was "Under the green tree" – yes, that was it. He said it several times, though he was almost unconscious, poor dear. "Under the green tree," he kept saying. I thought he meant something about where he was to be buried, so I asked the vicar if he could be laid at the shady end of the church-yard, near where the rest of the family were buried.

That's down in the village of course. And the vicar agreed, and I thought no more about it. But perhaps –'

'Yes?' said Richard eagerly, as Matty paused for a moment.

'Well, I've never thought of it before, but perhaps he meant something about the will. Perhaps he was trying to tell me where I should find the will.'

The same thought had leapt to Richard's mind almost before Matty had uttered it. He jumped up:

'I've got an idea,' he said. 'Do you mind if I go and look at Mr Jay's bedroom again? I suppose that's where he died?'

'Oh, yes,' said Matty. 'He was in bed there for several weeks before he passed away. It was his favourite room.'

Matty said he could go anywhere he liked, so bidding her good-bye, he hurried out of the room.

He found his way upstairs to old Mr Jay's bedroom, which Matty had shown them on their tour of inspection of the Manor. He glanced round the room, then crossed to the window and gazed out. A look of bewilderment came into his face. Then suddenly a light sprang into his eyes. At once he hurried downstairs and went to Matty's room.

'Miss Jay,' he said excitedly, 'what month did you say your brother died in?'

'It was February,' answered Matty promptly. 'I shall never forget it, because it was 14 February – Saint Valentine's Day, you know.'

'Oh, thank you, Miss Jay – thank you,' said Richard. 'Just what I wanted to know. I'll go and tell the others. Excuse me for a little while. I'll tell you later.'

He sped off towards the library.

'Poor boy,' said Matty, trying to close the lid of a suit-case with three coat-hangers and a pair of shoe-trees sticking out of one end, 'he's really quite mad, every bit as potty as I am. I daresay he knows what he's doing, though. Boys usually do.'

Chapter Seven

A SEARCH AND A MOVE

WHEN Richard got back to the library, he found Anne, Winston, and Deborah there. Beaver and Cherry had gone off to headquarters to get tea ready. Mrs Shipley's first-aid party had been relieved of further duties after scrubbing the kitchen floor and cleaning the oil-stove, and Mrs Shipley had sent Anne and the two boys out to play. She had been immensely impressed and cheered by their willing offer to help. In the library Anne and Winston were busily searching through some of the many remaining volumes. Deborah, who had been at it all the afternoon, was sitting at the painted bureau dreaming. The lid of it was open, and a pile of books lay in front of her. But in so far as she was thinking at all, it was the quaint pictures and decorations on the desk, rather than the unopened books, that held her attention.

'I say,' said Richard, bursting in excitedly, 'I've got an idea. Hullo – you back?' he said to Winston. 'Hullo, Anne. Where are the others?'

'Getting tea,' said Winston. 'It ought to be ready by now. Let's go and get it. What's all the excitement?'

'I'll tell you at H.Q.,' said Richard. 'Everyone's got to hear. Come on. Wake up, Deborah.'

But Deborah, pushing the picture of eighteenth-century shepherds and shepherdesses out of her mind, was already quite conscious. She got up and, joining the boys, went out through the french windows towards the paddock barn.

They climbed up into the two-wheeled dining-room and squeezed in as best they could. Food and drink were passed round; then Richard began.

'Look here,' he said, 'I've got an idea. It may be no go, but it's worth trying.'

'Well, spill it,' said Winston.

'Shut up,' said Beaver. 'It's probably a smashing idea.'

Richard ignored the interruptions and went on:

'It struck me that perhaps old Mr Jay didn't hide his will in the library at all, but somewhere else.'

'Oh yes,' said Cherry, 'under his mattress, or –'

'What about the priest's hole?' put in Deborah.

'Or he could have put it under a floor-board,' said Anne.

'Shall I go on?' asked Richard coldly, in the voice of a certain master at school. This was always an effective check on interruptions. There was silence immediately.

'Well, I asked Matty if her brother gave anything like a clue to where he might have put the will. You see, he never told her where it was, but towards the

77

end, when he knew he was most likely going to die, he tried to tell her. But he was too feeble to do it properly. Old people get like that, you know. Daddy says they go into a coma, or something. Anyway, he said several times something that sounded like "Under the green tree – under the green tree".'

'I see,' said Anne. 'You mean he hid it under a tree.'

'Perhaps,' said Richard. 'Of course he would have had to put it in a box or something and bury it, or it would have just blown away or rotted.'

'Well, let's go and look,' suggested Beaver. 'What are we waiting for?'

'The trouble is,' said Richard, 'the grounds are absolutely full of green trees. To begin with, there's the orchard, with plums, apples, cherries, and pears. There's the paddock and there's the garden.'

'Well, what are we going to do?' asked Anne. 'We can't look under every tree in the grounds.'

'I paid a visit to the old man's bedroom just now,' said Richard in his most Sherlock-Holmes-like manner. 'It is the room where he spent his last few weeks as an invalid and where he died. From his bed he could see all the far end of the paddock, including several green trees. The only thing is,' and here Richard paused for effect, '– the only thing is that in January and February, when the old man was ill, the trees weren't green. Most of them would be quite brown.'

The others were most impressed. Then Deborah spoke:

'But what about evergreens?' she said. 'You know – the holly and the ivy.'

'Exactly,' said Richard. 'Not quite all the trees would be brown in February. So I looked out of Mr

Jay's bedroom window to see if there were any ever-greens in view. There were two – a big holly-bush and a tall thing something like a cedar and something like a cypress. I think it's a cypress of some sort, but I don't know. Personally, if the will is hidden under either of them, I think it would be the cypress thing. If it had been the other, he'd have said "Under the holly-tree", not "Under the green tree", because he would have known the name. Anyway, the holly isn't so much a tree as a bush.'

'It's worth trying,' said Winston. They were all rather favourably struck by Richard's cleverness.

'Let's go and see,' someone said. 'Come on.'

'No,' said Richard. 'Put away the tea-things first, and tidy up.'

It took them less than two minutes to tidy away the tea-things. Then they ran out to the far end of the paddock.

As Richard had said, the only evergreens within sight of Mr Jay's bedroom window were a large, over-grown holly-bush and a tall, dark-leaved tree, perhaps a yew or a cypress. Its trunk was fairly straight, though old and gnarled. There was no hollow in which any-thing could be hidden. But the roots were twisted, knotted, and snake-like, leaving plenty of cavities underneath, into which a packet could be thrust. They bent down and rummaged, but nothing was found.

'You know,' said Richard, 'he wouldn't just have stuffed it into a hole; he would have buried it properly, if this was his hiding-place.'

'Don't see why he should bury it at all,' said Win-ston, who was not looking forward to the task of up-rooting such a formidable obstacle. 'Seems crazy to me.'

'Yes, but the old man did do crazy things,' said Richard. 'It's just the sort of thing he might do.'

'That's right,' said Beaver.

'Well, you dig up the tree and have a look,' said Winston.

'All right. I don't mind,' retorted Beaver staunchly.

'Come on, then,' said Richard. 'Let's get some tools from the shed.'

They found a spade, two forks (one of them with a broken prong), a pick-axe, and a crow-bar. For a quarter of an hour nothing was to be heard but the occasional clink of iron on a buried flint and the heavy breathing of the excavators as they toiled in the afternoon sun. Everyone took a turn, even Cherry. Every few minutes she proclaimed her certainty that she had struck a treasure-chest, but alas! the only thing she struck was poor Beaver, but he took it cheerfully. When half an hour had passed, and the ground for yards round the base of the tree was pitted and scored by the children's efforts, they began to show signs of discouragement. Winston went and investigated the holly-bush, but it presented a severe problem. It was impossible to get near the roots of the holly without having your head, neck, and hands badly pricked.

'Look here,' he said. 'I vote two of us go on with the books. That's still the best chance, if you ask me. We haven't tried half of them yet. There's thousands to look at still.'

'All right,' agreed Richard. 'You and Anne and Cherry go on with the books, and Beaver and I will go on digging. Which do you want to do, Deborah?'

'I'll dig a bit more if you like,' said Deborah.

'I want to stay with Richard,' piped Cherry.

'All right,' said Deborah. 'I'll go back to the library, and you stay here, Cherry.'

So three went back to the library and the other three stayed in the paddock and excavated.

When it was time to go home, many papers had accumulated on the table, and much good black earth had piled up round the tree, and several hands were blistered, but there was still no sign of the last will and testament of the late Stephen Jay.

That evening the weather broke, and Mrs Shipley woke up with a fit of coughing to hear thunder rolling out over the sea. The sky was lit with sudden pale lightning flashes in the distance. She had a restless night, and was only too glad next morning to find her first-aid party at the door, ready to do anything she asked. Deborah went shopping with Anne, and

Richard and Cherry industriously swept and polished the living-room, peeled the potatoes, and laid the table for dinner.

In the afternoon the search continued at the Manor. There was no more digging, at any rate for the time being. The storm had brought heavy rain, and the tall evergreen was surrounded by mud. All the same, Richard had not quite given up his idea. The phrase 'Under the green tree' stuck in his head, and kept repeating itself at intervals.

Miss Jay, meanwhile, went steadily on with her packing; at last she had reduced the chaos in her room to something like order, and an array of cases and baskets lay ready to be taken by taxi to her new lodging in the village. So long as there was a chance of finding the will, she was not going to leave the Manor altogether; she would go there by day and see that the children had all they wanted, and attend to much that still remained to do there. But she had promised her friend, the widowed Mrs Mosscrop, to move into her guest-house as soon as possible, and help with the holiday visitors. The packing was scarcely finished when the one and only Mulbridge taxi crunched its way up the Manor drive and jolted to a standstill outside the front door. All the children came out to see Miss Jay off. She and the cases were all bundled in somehow, and room was found for the protesting Dennis, who did not want to go for a ride, but who refused to be parted from his adored mistress.

'It would be so nice,' said Miss Jay, 'if one of you would care to come down to the village with me and help with the luggage. I don't know quite how you're going to get in, but perhaps you could squeeze in somehow on top of the things.'

'I'll come,' said Richard, 'but I'll bike down. Then I'll have the bike to come back here on.'

'Can I come, Richard?' asked Cherry.

'No, you stay this time,' said her brother. 'I won't be long. What about you coming too, Deborah?'

So Richard and Deborah set off on their bicycles, and were out of the drive before the ancient taxi could turn round, start up, and overtake them. Winston was left in charge of the search-party. Mrs Shipley had said she could do without help that afternoon, as everything necessary had been done in the morning.

Richard and Deborah sped along the gravel road only a little way behind the taxi. They crossed the heath and began descending the hill that skirted the dark recesses of Mulbridge Woods. Here they were able to overtake the taxi, as Miss Jay made it stop while the driver obligingly posted some letters of hers in the little pillar-box beside the road. They reached 'Rosebank', the abode of Mrs Mosscrop, on the outskirts of Mulbridge, almost at the same moment as the taxi.

'Rosebank, Private Guest-House, Luncheons and Teas provided for Non-Residents' is a tall, plain house whose plainness is somewhat redeemed by the blazing geraniums and luxuriant hydrangeas in the garden, and by the lilac and laburnum that bloom each summer. Why anyone should come and stay in Mulbridge is something of a mystery; but the house is a comfortable, easy-going one for people who do not like too much fuss and formality, and the country round is pleasant. The sea is not far off, the garden is quiet and shady, Mrs Mosscrop's cooking has acquired a favourable reputation among certain unadventurous visitors, who have become regular summer arrivals.

There are always motor-cyclists, cyclists, and walkers who need lunch or tea in the summer months. Indeed, this particular summer Mrs Mosscrop was so overwhelmed with visitors, resident or casual, that she was only too glad of Matty's energetic, if erratic, assistance. Matty, for her part, was glad to have work to do now that her brother was dead; moreover, she had never been well off and was by now in need of money, since nothing would be forthcoming from the estate until the will could be found and proved. Not that Mrs Mosscrop would pay her, but she would charge nothing for board and lodging, so long as Matty helped with the meals.

Richard and Deborah left their cycles outside the gate and assisted Matty up the stairs with her numerous bags and baskets. Mrs Mosscrop had managed to keep for her friend a small but pleasant room overlooking the garden, and here the luggage was stowed. True, the room was on the second floor, but Matty assured Mrs Mosscrop she had a good heart and did not mind stairs.

The proprietress of 'Rosebank' guest-house was fat, jolly, and bustling.

'Who are you?' she asked Richard, as he and Deborah came in with the last two bags. Richard explained.

'Miss Jay and I are going to have a cup of tea in my sitting-room just now,' she went on. 'You'd better have some too. Any friend of Matty's is a friend of mine. I dare say you can manage some home-made scones and a bit of strawberry jam and perhaps a cream bun? Or perhaps you don't like such things! Never can tell with you young people nowadays.'

Very soon they were seated in Mrs Mosscrop's

comfortable cretonne-covered armchairs partaking of
the dainties she had mentioned. It was early for tea,
but Mrs Mosscrop had to be ready for the residents'
and the casuals' tea-time at four o'clock. The sky was
overcast, so that today there would be no tea in the
garden, and stray visitors would probably be few. Ivy,
the tireless maid-of-all-work, could start them off, so
Mrs Mosscrop and Matty settled down for a nice
heart-to-heart talk about everything and everybody in
the world.

When they had eaten all they could, despite their
hostess's continued pressure to have just one more
cake, the two children said they had better be getting
back to their friends.

'Right ho,' said Mrs Mosscrop cheerily. 'If you say
so. Sure you won't have just one more cream bun,
young man? Ah well, young men aren't what they
used to be. Good-bye. Come and see me again, won't
you? I expect you can find your own way out.'

They thanked her profusely, left the sitting-room,
and closed the door behind them. The door of the tea-
room opposite was ajar. As Richard glanced in, something caught his eye. He touched Deborah's arm and
signalled to her to look inside the room. She did so.

'See that?' said Richard in a whisper.

'Why, it's Seedy!' exclaimed Deborah.

'Yes,' said Richard. 'Be quiet, though. Don't let
him catch us staring at him.'

Tea had just begun, and over in the far corner of the
room sat the seedy man whom they had seen gazing at
Dragon in the paddock. He was not alone. A small,
fat, dusty man sat beside him. Over the tea-cups they
were deep in conversation.

'Fancy finding him in a place like this,' said Richard.

'I should have thought he'd feel more at home in a snack-bar. Wonder who the dusty-looking gent is. Perhaps he wants to buy horses too.'

'Come on, Richard,' whispered Deborah. 'We can't stay here.'

Just then Ivy came from the kitchen with a tray of tea-things.

'Do you want tea?' she said to the children.

'No, thank you,' said Richard. 'We've just had tea with Mrs Mosscrop. I say, can you tell us who that man over there in the corner is? I'm sure I've seen him somewhere before.'

Richard had stepped back so that the seedy man could not catch sight of him. Ivy looked across the room at the stranger's table.

'Couldn't say,' she answered. 'He's not a resident. Just dropped in for tea, like. We get all sorts here holiday times. Excuse me – I've got work to do.'

So saying, she pushed her way through the door and disappeared among the tea-tables.

The children were surprised to find the seedy man at 'Rosebank'. They would have been even more surprised had they known what he was at that moment saying to his dusty companion. But both strangers were soon forgotten in the exertion of the ride uphill along the quiet, unfrequented lane towards the heath. All was still and peaceful – so still that the birds in Mulbridge Woods, refreshed by the night's rain, seemed to be singing more piercingly and more sweetly than ever.

Back at headquarters Richard noted the events of the past two days briefly in his journal – the appearance of Seedy in the paddock, Matty's revelation about her brother's dying words, the fruitless search under the

A SEARCH AND A MOVE

tree, the 'home help' scheme for Mrs Shipley, and finally Matty's move to 'Rosebank'. He concluded with the words:

'No nearer to finding S.J.'s will. Shall we ever succeed?'

Chapter Eight

'SHALL WE EVER SUCCEED?'

RICHARD did not say anything to the others about his growing doubts. But another two days passed, hundreds more books were searched, and still there was no will. Winston and Deborah took a day off; they had a chance to go to the sea for the day. Cherry came because her brother came, but she had long ceased to turn the pages of old Mr Jay's dusty volumes. Anne and Beaver continued the search faithfully, but they began to wonder whether they were not simply wasting time. Still, headquarters was a delightful refuge, and they continued to appear cheerful and hopeful. The Manor was not the same now that Matty had moved, even though she came each day and pottered about, doing this and that in the great house, and occasionally coming into the library to lend a hand.

If only they could *do* something, Richard thought. Chasing bandits, exploring caves in the cliffs, or decoding secret documents – anything like that would have been exciting; but this endless flipping over the pages of dull books was no work for heroes, or even for ordinary boys and girls.

There was no more digging in the paddock. This was felt to be a hopeless waste of time – at least as long as any more books remained unturned.

'Come on,' said Richard, lifting down half a dozen heavy volumes of *The Collected Works of John Ruskin*, 'let's try this lot.'

But Anne could tell he was getting discouraged.

'Don't give up, Richard,' she said. She thought of her poor mother lying peacefully upstairs in the sunny room she had chosen for her. 'Matty's terribly keen on keeping the house – I mean, letting it be a hospital. I'll never give up.'

'Who's talking about giving up? My father's a doctor, so I know only too well how much we need a hospital round here. All the same, I can't help wondering whether we're on the right lines. A man who had all these books wouldn't be such an absolute fool as to leave such an important thing just in any old book, would he?'

'I don't know. Matty said he might.'

'"Under the green tree,"' said Richard. '"Under the green tree." Wonder if the old man meant anything by it.'

'More digging?' put in Beaver hopefully. He much preferred digging the ground to digging in books.

'No,' said Richard. 'I've had enough spade-work for the present.'

'It's like a song we did at school last term,' said Anne. '"Under the greenwood tree" – it goes like this.'

She sang a few bars in her clear treble voice.

'That's an idea,' said Richard. '"Under the green-*wood* tree." Perhaps that's what he said. Let's ask Matty.'

As if in answer to his suggestion, in came Matty a moment later with a tray of biscuits and lemonade.

'I thought you'd like something to revive your drooping spirits,' she said. 'Jolly dusty work, I dare say. Do you think we ought to give it up? Oh, I do hope not; but I'm afraid it's terribly dull for you.'

The children accepted the refreshments gratefully,

and Richard, ignoring any suggestion that the search should be abandoned, asked:

'I say, Miss Jay, do you think your brother could have said "Under the green*wood* tree", not just "Under the green tree"?'

Matty considered this.

'He *might*,' she said. 'He might easily. I have a very poor memory, you know. But how would it help?'

'There's a song called "Under the greenwood tree",' went on Richard. 'Do you know who wrote the words?'

'Milton, I think,' said Matty, 'or it might have been Wordsworth. He was always writing about trees and things of that sort. Very fond of nature, he was. You might find it in some book of poetry.'

'Yes,' said Richard. 'Here we are – *The Oxford Book of English Verse*. Let's have a look. "Index of First Lines." Here it is – "Under the greenwood tree, No. 135".'

Rapidly he turned the pages until he came to No. 135. Perhaps he was half hoping the will would fall out when he opened the book at the poem. But no such thing happened.

'It's by Shakespeare,' he said.

'Of course it is,' said Matty. 'Isn't that what I said? Or did I say Milton? I can't remember.'

'Which play does it come in?' pursued Richard. 'You said Mr Jay was fond of reading Shakespeare.'

'Oh, he was,' affirmed Matty. 'He loved Shakespeare. Look, he has a whole shelf full of Shakespeare's plays.'

'And we haven't touched them yet. Come on, let's have them out.'

'Now I come to think of it,' said Matty, 'I believe

it's a song from *As You Like It*. We must have done it at school. I read the part of Rosalind, though you'd hardly believe it.'

Matty was right for once. The song does indeed come from *As You Like It*, and Mr Jay had several editions of this play. Each one was searched in turn, then the whole of Shakespeare's works were examined, but once more without results. Only an old book bill, two or three theatre programmes, a newspaper cutting, and a couple of private letters of no interest lurked in the pages of Shakespeare.

'Oh, well,' Richard said cheerfully, 'another good idea gone wrong. Never mind – third time lucky.'

'Poor Richard,' said Anne. 'My fault, really, I suppose, for thinking of that silly song. I shall never like it again.'

But the suggestion was perhaps not so silly as she had thought. That evening Richard was in the sitting-room at home with his mother and father, who were vainly trying to persuade him to go to bed. They were listening to the radio.

'Now come on,' his father said. 'Variety programme's finished, and it's time you were off.'

'All right,' said Richard reluctantly, getting to his feet. He was about to kiss his mother good night and leave the room, when his ears were caught by the opening announcement of the next programme:

'This is the B.B.C. Home Service,' the gentleman at Broadcasting House was saying. 'The time is eight-thirty, and our next programme is the first part of a dramatized version of the novel by Thomas Hardy – *Under the Greenwood Tree*. The part of –'

'I say, switch off the wireless before you go,' said his father. 'I've got some work to do.'

Richard did as he was asked, but he had heard all he needed. 'The novel by Thomas Hardy, *Under the Greenwood Tree*.' Well, that was something else to go on. He tried to remember whether it was a book they had already looked at, but how could he possibly recall the titles of some thousands of books, most of which he had not even read?

Next morning he and Cherry called for the Joneses, and Deborah and Cherry and he went to do their share of housework for Anne's mother. Mrs Shipley was feeling better, and she had been cheered by a letter from her husband in Portsmouth to say that the job there finished at the end of the week, and he would be at home for a bit. Nevertheless, the children insisted on dusting and polishing, cleaning shoes, peeling potatoes, and doing the shopping.

In the afternoon, Richard and Deborah went straight to the library. He had told her about *Under the Greenwood Tree*, and Deborah had noticed some books by Thomas Hardy on a shelf they had not yet investigated.

'"The Wessex Edition of the Novels of Thomas Hardy,"' Richard read. '*Tess of the D'Urbervilles*, *Jude the Obscure*, *A Pair of Blue Eyes*, *Two on a Tower*.'

But where was *Under the Greenwood Tree*? This was not the only one of Hardy's novels that was missing. By looking at the complete list at the beginning of one of the volumes, they were able to discover that there were at least half a dozen which the shelf did not contain. Either Mr Jay had never had them, or else they were lost or sold.

They went in search of Matty to see if she could help.

'She's a nice old thing,' said Richard, 'but I wish she wasn't so vague.'

They found her in the orchard, perched perilously on a kitchen chair, gathering plums.

At Richard's request she descended to answer inquiries.

'Do you know if Mr Jay had *all* the novels of Thomas Hardy – including *Under the Greenwood Tree*?' asked Richard.

'Goodness me, what questions you ask,' said Matty. 'But indeed he must have done. He was very keen on Hardy, you know. As a matter of fact, he knew Hardy slightly – by correspondence of course. I think Hardy gave him copies of one or two of his books. Stephen was most flattered. He had presentation copies of books by all sorts of writers. Arnold Bennett was one and I *think* George Moore gave him *Esther Waters*, or would it be –'

'Yes, yes,' said Richard excitedly. 'But did he give him *Under the Greenwood Tree*? And if so, where is it?'

'Ah, that I don't know,' said Matty. 'Have a plum. That's right. Take several. They'll only go bad, you know – and you'd better take some for Anne's mother.'

'*Please*,' begged Richard, 'please try to think – could your brother have *sold* any of his books by Hardy?'

'Oh yes, I dare say he might,' said Matty. 'I see what you are driving at. I know he *did* sell books from time to time – quite valuable ones sometimes. You see, we were often hard up for ready money, and he had *so* many books. You know, I think he must have had several thousand – the library is *full* of them! But of course you know all about *that*, poor things, don't you?'

'If he sold them, where would he sell them?' asked Richard.

'Well, he might post them off to Oxford or London,' said Matty, 'but as often as not he would take them to Mr Flaxman in Mulcaster.'

They thanked Matty for the plums and the information and hurried back to the library. They had already noticed a number of gaps among the books, and had supposed this was due simply to their having got out of order. But now it seemed more than likely that these were caused by books having been taken out to be sold.

Richard sat down among the papers which had piled up on the centre table.

'Here,' he said, 'help sort these out. If you see any bills or receipts from booksellers, see if any of them say anything about books sold.'

They found a number of bills from booksellers in

Bournemouth, Oxford, Cambridge, and London. Some of them contained the item: 'By credit', followed by a sum of money. Evidently this represented an allowance made by the bookseller for books which Mr Jay had sold to him. But no names of books were mentioned, and no reference was discovered to any book by Hardy.

'I'm going out,' said Richard decisively. 'I've got an idea, but it may be no good. Go on looking, and when the others come, have tea as usual. If I'm not back, don't wait. Deborah, you're in charge. Look after Cherry, won't you? Winston or you can see that she gets home, can't you?'

There were questions and protests, but Richard hardly waited to hear them. He was off on his bicycle, across the heath in the direction of Mulcaster, almost before they realized he had gone.

Richard sped along the road towards the city. His idea was fantastic, but perhaps not hopeless. So fantastic was it that he had not dared tell the others what it was. Yet it seemed to him well worth while to find out if there was a chance of recovering the dead book-collector's copy of *Under the Greenwood Tree* – if, that was, he had ever possessed one. Could it be that the old man would actually have sold the very book containing the will? It was scarcely possible; yet Matty had spoken of their being short of ready cash sometimes, and perhaps she herself had sold the book, without knowing its importance. He wished he had thought of asking her. Still, ten to one she would not remember. Then again, if the book he was looking for was a presentation copy, from the author, would Mr Jay have been likely to sell it? But perhaps it was *not* this one that Hardy had presented to him. Perhaps it

was another. At least he could see what Mr Flaxman
had to say.

He left his bicycle outside the bookshop and went in.
The door-bell jangled. He went through the outer
shop, which was kept for new books, into the second-
hand department behind. He knew Mr Flaxman, a
short-sighted and somewhat short-tempered old gentleman, to whom books were treasures and customers
something of a nuisance. However, it was not Mr
Flaxman who greeted him, but his wife.

'I want to inquire about some second-hand books,'
Richard began.

'What a pity!' said the bookseller's wife. 'My
husband is out. He's gone to a sale. *He* deals with
second-hand books – I don't really know anything
about them. But you can look round if you like. The
prices are marked.'

'I really want to speak to Mr Flaxman himself.
When will he be back?'

'What's the time? Four o'clock. He should be back
soon – I expect him about five. Could you come back
then?'

There was nothing for it but to put up with the
delay. Richard went home, had a hasty tea, and got
back to the shop as the cathedral clock was striking
five.

Mr Flaxman had just got in.

'What can I do for you, Mr Masters?' he asked,
looking at Richard over his steel-rimmed spectacles.

'It's like this,' began Richard. 'Only please don't
tell anyone, as it's something rather secret. You won't
tell, will you?'

'How can I tell anything when I don't know what
there is to tell?' asked Mr Flaxman.

Richard explained that for a special reason he wanted to recover old Mr Jay's copy of *Under the Greenwood Tree*. He begged Mr Flaxman not to ask why. Mr Flaxman said that he had known the old man well, and that he had been grieved to hear of his death.

'Oh yes, he often used to come in here – in the old days, that is, before he found it difficult to get about, he bought a lot of books here. He was a good customer. I often used to find him something that these clever London fellows couldn't lay a hand on for love nor money. But how do you expect me to remember everything he bought or sold in my shop?'

'Oh, please, Mr Flaxman,' said Richard earnestly, 'do try to remember. It's very important.'

'Let me think. Hardy, you say – *Under the Greenwood Tree*. I certainly can't remember his having sold me a copy. As a matter of fact, I doubt if I'd have bought it, even if he'd offered me it. I've usually several copies in stock.'

'Can I look at them?' said Richard.

'Certainly, if you wish. But I'm positive none of them belonged to the late Mr Jay.'

And so it proved. Mr Flaxman had three copies of Hardy's novel, but none of them had Mr Jay's name in it, nor did any document slip out of the pages when Richard accidentally dropped one copy and casually turned the leaves of the others.

'I tell you what,' said Mr Flaxman. 'You're a bit of a nuisance, but I can see you won't be happy till you've found the book.'

'Oh, I'm sorry, Mr Fl—'

'Don't interrupt, if you please. Look here – when customers bring in books I don't want to buy, I usually send them on to old Jacobus in Market Street. You know him, I've no doubt. Deals in antiques and junk of all sorts. Has a few shelves of books, too. Not much, of course – nothing like mine – but he's not so fussy about what he buys, and he doesn't give such good prices – nor get them, I'll be bound.'

The bookseller chuckled, as if admiring his own skill as a dealer in second-hand books.

'Old Mr Jay often used to go to Jacobus. I should try him if I were you.'

'Oh, I will,' said Richard. 'Do you know when he closes?'

'Half past five, I should think, like most of us – and quite late enough, if you ask me. Now run along and don't keep me talking.'

Richard thanked Mr Flaxman, but the bookseller had already stumped off among his bookcases.

As he left the shop and mounted his bicycle, the youthful detective, absorbed though he was, could not help noticing someone idly looking into the window of the shop opposite. It was the short, dusty gentleman who had been in conversation with Seedy in the tea-room at 'Rosebank' the day Matty had moved in. As Richard pedalled off rapidly in the direction of Market Street, the dusty man, suddenly losing his air of idleness, stepped briskly across the road and began walking with remarkable speed, considering his build, in the direction that Richard had taken.

Chapter Nine

AN INTRUDER
AT HEADQUARTERS

RICHARD hardly had time to speculate on the presence of the dusty man before he found himself at the antique shop in Market Street. It was, indeed, only just round the corner from Mr Flaxman's. As he dismounted, Mr Jacobus, the antique dealer, emerged from his front door and was about to begin putting his shutters up for the night. But he was a friend of Richard's. Many a time he had found him an old fencing foil or a broken alarm clock among the humbler articles in his back room.

'Oh, Mr Jacobus,' said Richard breathlessly. 'Don't shut up shop for a minute. Wait for me, please!'

'It's all right,' said the antique dealer, 'I'm a few minutes early. Want to come in and have a look round?'

'I want to ask you something,' said Richard, 'something rather special.'

'Come inside then. I can leave the shop open for a few minutes. Will it take long?'

'No, I don't think so – that is, it all depends.'

Richard followed Mr Jacobus into the shop. The dealer was a kindly man, elderly, grey-suited, and slow in movement. Everything about him was rather faded, except his two very sharp eyes.

'Now, what's it all about?' he asked, as soon as the door had closed behind them. 'If you want to buy the Crown Jewels, well, I just can't help you. But –'

Richard laughed.

'No,' he said, 'it's not jewels, Mr Jacobus. It's books. Please don't ask what for just now – I'll tell you all about it later if – that is, if everything comes out all right, but what I want to know is – did old Mr Jay ever come in here – you know, Mr Jay who died last winter at Mulbridge Manor?'

'Why, yes, to be sure. Often came in here, did old Stephen Jay. I knew him before you were born.'

'Did he ever sell you any books?'

'Yes, indeed – *and* bought them too. Not often, mind you, because I don't specialize in books. But sometimes he picked up an oddment or two from the shelves, and sometimes he brought in a few volumes for disposal.'

'Have you any of his books now, by any chance? Or can you remember the names of any of them? Oh, please, try to remember – it's most important.'

'You *do* want to know something, you do!' said Mr Jacobus. 'Why, he hadn't been in here for a twelve-month before he died. But you know, I've a very good memory, and I'm pretty sure he dropped in about the Christmas before last – or perhaps a couple of months before Christmas – with a parcel of books that Flax-man had no use for. But what they *were* I can't recall. Was there any particular book you were interested in?'

During this conversation Mr Jacobus had turned his observant eyes more than once towards the window, into which, for perhaps a minute and a half, the dusty gentleman had been gazing. He appeared to be intensely interested in an old ivory chess set whose red and white figures were indeed fascinating. Richard had often stopped to look at them himself. But now

the dusty man stepped resolutely to the door, opened
it, and entered the shop.

'Anything I can do for you?' asked Mr Jacobus.

'Mind if I look round?' asked Dusty casually.

'I'm just shutting shop. We close at five-thirty, you
know, so if there's nothing special, you might come
back tomorrow. We open at nine.'

'Can't come tomorrow,' said Dusty. 'I'll just look
round till you shut the shop.'

'I'm shutting it this minute,' said Mr Jacobus very
firmly. 'My young friend and I have something to discuss, and we can do it just as well with the shutters up.
So if you don't *mind* –'

Dusty hesitated, as if wondering whether to make a

scene; but there was something in the dealer's manner which discouraged him.

'Have it your own way,' he muttered sulkily, and shuffled out of the door. Mr Jacobus followed him into the street and resolutely put up the shutters, determined to have no further interruption. He returned to the shop, which was now dark, switched on the light, and said:

'I don't suppose I've lost a very valuable customer in *him* – just hanging around, you know. I get a lot of them. You can always tell whether they're really interested in anything. Well, now, where are we?'

Richard had been wondering how much to tell the antique dealer. But it was no good trying to make a complete secret of it.

'I want to find Mr Jay's copy of *Under the Greenwood Tree*,' he said. 'You see, it may – it just *may* contain an important paper, one that Miss Jay, his sister, you know – particularly wants. I suppose you can't remember if he sold you *Under the Greenwood Tree*?'

'Thomas Hardy, isn't it? Great admirer of Hardy was Stephen Jay. I remember he picked up a first edition of *Tess* here. My word, he was pleased! Now, let me see.'

He thought deeply for a few moments, while Richard waited anxiously.

'Why, yes,' he said at length. 'I think there may have been some of Hardy's novels among the books he brought in that time. It's just possible – in fact, now I come to think of it, it's more than likely. I couldn't swear to it, but I wouldn't be surprised.'

'I suppose you can't remember if there were any loose papers in it?' asked Richard eagerly.

'Now you're asking too much,' said the dealer with

finality. 'I don't get time to look through all the books that are brought in. I just price them and push them into the shelves.'

'Isn't it still there?' asked Richard.

'No, that it isn't,' said Mr Jacobus. 'I turn out my stock pretty fast – in the matter of books, anyway. But in this case, I've a fair idea who might have bought it.'

'Oh, who?' asked Richard.

It seemed impossible that even if he found the missing book, the will would still be there; but sometimes a wild chance was worth taking.

'Do you know Miss Anstey-Farthing, down at the Mill House?' the dealer asked.

'No,' said Richard, 'but I know who you mean. Isn't she the lady who pops about on a little motorbike – one of those bicycles with a sort of outboard motor?'

'That's right,' answered Mr Jacobus. 'You've got it. I thought everyone knew Miss Anstey-Farthing. Dear old thing she is. Always looking in here for odd things – books sometimes, coins too, or medals, and only last week she wanted an old Victorian backscratcher. Never know what she'll ask for next. Well, you try her! I've a pretty good idea she may have bought the Hardy novels belonging to Stephen Jay – that is, if there *were* any Hardy novels. If she can't help you, come back and have another talk. Perhaps I can think of someone else. But it's my belief she's got your book, if anyone has.'

Richard thanked Mr Jacobus cordially. The dealer waved aside his thanks and showed him the side door.

'I've no idea what you're up to,' he said, 'but I won't ask questions. Good luck to you. By the way, tell your father I've a half dozen William and Mary silver teaspoons if he still wants them.'

'I will,' said Richard, 'and thanks awfully, Mr Jacobus. I *must* go now. Good-bye.'

Richard slipped out into a passage leading back into Market Street, mounted his bicycle, and rode off thoughtfully. How he was going to approach the famous Miss Anstey-Farthing he could not imagine. In any case, he would have to put it off till the next day. Mill House was some distance away, and it was too late to go there this evening. Besides, he must think of some excuse for calling. She was not one of his father's patients – of that, Richard was certain. It was probable that she had no doctor. An old lady who chugged about on a motor-cycle at a quite respectable speed was obviously no weakling. He knew nobody who knew her, either. He had an idea that she had once given away the prizes at his school, but that would not be of much help. He could ask his father what to do, but that would mean explanations. In any case, what was he going to say to the lady herself? He was puzzling over this problem when he reached home, to find that Cherry had just been delivered safely by Winston Jones.

'I had a lovely ride with Winston,' said Cherry. 'He simply whizzed like the wind. *Much* faster than you go.'

'Well, you'd better not tell Daddy,' said Richard coldly, annoyed by his sister's comparison. 'You know he's not at all keen on you riding on cycle-carriers.'

'Winston said I was to tell you,' said Cherry, ignoring Richard's suggestion, 'they're all going to the Manor in the morning tomorrow. Anne's mummy says she can do without help. She's feeling better. So will you come?'

'I don't know,' said Richard. 'I've got something important to do.'

'Oh, what?' asked Cherry. 'Where are you going? Do take me! I don't mind even if you *are* a slowcoach on your bike.'

'That's jolly decent of you, I'm sure,' said Richard.

'I'll see. It all depends. You'd better go into the kitchen now and get your supper, or they'll say you've been kept up late. Then you won't come *at all – any more*. See!'

This tragic possibility silenced Cherry, and she did as she was told.

Next morning, as soon as his mother was safely upstairs making beds and his father had driven off to the hospital, Richard went into the consulting-room and opened the local telephone directory.

'Here we are – "Anstey-Farthing, Miss V".' He picked up the telephone and asked for the number.

A voice answered. It was a woman's voice and sounded foreign.

''Oo is it?' asked the voice. 'No. Miss Anstey-Farthing is not 'ome. Yes, she will be in to –'

At this point the speaker, whoever it was, was interrupted by a high-pitched yapping.

'Quiet, Mahjong – lie down! Sorry,' the voice continued, 'very sorry. It is the dog. She will be in to lunch. Is there any message? Very well – you come after lunch. Yes. Yes, I tell her. Good-bye.'

There was nothing for it but to put off his visit to the lady at Mill House until after lunch. She would be out most of the morning, probably terrorizing the countryside on her absurd motor-bike.

A number of odd jobs kept him at home for half an hour or so, until Cherry's impatience to be off finally prevailed.

'Come on, Richard,' she said. 'They'll be waiting for us. I 'spect they've found the will by now.'

'I hope they have,' said Richard. 'All right, Cherry Blossom. I'm ready now. Let's be going.'

They pedalled soberly through Mulcaster in the morning sunshine, and climbed the long hill to the heath. Once more it looked like being a perfect day. There were only a few hundred books left to be searched. Surely this was going to be their lucky day. Richard had very little hope of Miss Anstey-Farthing and the copy of *Under the Greenwood Tree*, which she might or might not have bought second-hand from Mr Jacobus. If she still had the book in her possession there was very little chance that the will would be among its pages, even supposing it had ever been put there. And what person in his senses, old and scatter-brained though he might be, would go and sell a book containing such a precious paper? It was not as if he could have forgotten he had put it there, for the very reason why Richard was searching for that particular book was that it *might* have been mentioned to Miss Jay by the old man on his death-bed. Of course he might have temporarily forgotten it was in the book. But was it likely? There were altogether too many 'mights' in the story. Still, Richard had started on the quest of the missing novel, and he was not going to give it up, however fantastic it seemed.

When he and Cherry reached the Manor, they found Winston scouting for them at the gates. He was looking anxious.

'Oh, here you are,' he said. 'Where on earth have you been all this time? I say, something's happened.'

Without offering any further explanation, he hurried off in the direction of headquarters, while the two newcomers followed close behind.

Deborah, Anne, and Beaver were waiting at the entrance to the barn.

'Look inside,' said Winston. 'We got here about an hour ago. We've left it for you to see – just as we found it.'

Richard stepped inside the barn and waited a few moments to accustom his eyes to the comparative darkness. Then he said:

'Hullo! What on earth have you been up to?'

The trestle council table had been overturned. The box underneath was open, the straw 'sofa' seemed to have been scattered to the winds, and the seats of the pony-trap, which they used as a larder, had been opened and the contents thrown about in disorder. Richard examined the chaos, noticing particularly that his private journal was missing from its usual place.

'Somebody's been here,' said Winston. 'This is exactly how we found it.'

'Could it have been the dog?' asked Richard.

'Shouldn't think so,' said Deborah. 'Dennis would never rummage about like this and knock the table over.'

'He might,' said Richard, 'if Matty forgot to feed him. Perhaps he was looking for food.'

'Food's still there,' said Winston. 'There was only a bread-loaf, some stale sandwiches, half a pot of jam and a tin of biscuits, and they're still there. In fact, nothing's missing – except the journal.'

'Have you looked for it?' asked Richard.

'Yes. It's gone.'

'Well, let's have another look.'

For some time they all searched here and there, rummaging through the straw, searching in corners, and even in the long grass of the paddock, but the journal was nowhere to be found.

'Some tramp, I should think,' ventured Beaver.

'Gipsies perhaps,' said Winston.

'That seedy fellow, more likely,' said Richard, 'or –'

He paused, remembering the interest which Dusty had shown in his movements the evening before among the shops of Mulcaster. But the others did not yet know about that. Perhaps he had better tell them.

'Well, let's put this straight,' he said.

They did not take long to restore order to their rudely disarranged headquarters. What was troubling them all was that someone unknown to them was obviously beginning to show too much interest in their activities. Of course it might have been some chance intruder, but it was very odd that, while the provisions had been left untouched, the journal of their proceedings should have disappeared. Supposing someone interested in the late Mr Jay's will had actually taken the journal, how much would he learn from it? Not very much, perhaps, for after all there was not very much to be kept secret. Richard had certainly noted down his idea about the book named *Under the Greenwood Tree* and its connexion with what Miss Jay thought her dying brother had said. For the rest, the children themselves knew no more than the intruder did about the missing will.

When everything was once more in its place, Richard summoned a council meeting and told them of his visits to the second-hand bookshop and to Mr Jacobus's antique shop, of the suspicious behaviour of Dusty, and of the proposed visit to Miss Anstey-Farthing at Mill House. He had just concluded his story when Miss Jay appeared at the barn door in a state of agitation. Dennis, too, shared his mistress's distress, running this way and that and sniffing excitedly.

'I've just had a letter,' she said. 'It came this morning. It's from my nephew's lawyer in London. He says that Gerald intends to take immediate possession of the Manor, and that if there is a will – which he very much doubts – it must be produced at once, or there is nothing to prevent Gerald from becoming the legal owner. We must find it at once,' continued Matty,

'– at once. There's not a day to be lost. My brother couldn't have borne that Gerald should get the Manor. He *always* said that I was to have it. The hospital is needed so badly. Oh, you *will* do what you can, won't you?'

Chapter Ten

AN INCIDENT IN MILL LANE

OF course the children agreed to return to the search
with redoubled zest. Once more they settled down in
the library and brought down bundles of the remaining
books from the upper shelves. Richard, alas, had under-
estimated the number. Even with everyone helping,
there was at least a further two days' work. Moreover,
Winston and Deborah had an idea about a hiding-place
under the floor, and Beaver had been detailed to go all
over the house in search of loose boards. The priest's
hole was searched, but to no effect; other rooms were
tried, one or two loose boards were prised up, but
nothing was found beneath them except dust and
rubble.

Then there were the attics, a hitherto unexplored
hiding-place for junk of all descriptions – not merely
boxes and broken furniture, rusty fire-irons and disused household utensils of every sort, but old books
and bundles of papers; and the papers had to be gone
through – hastily, but not too casually, for fear the
precious document should be overlooked. Matty herself helped, but her eagerness to find the will did not
prevent her from wasting valuable time re-reading old
letters and scanning the pages of books she had loved
as a child.

The urgency of the situation caused a slight change
of plan. Richard was wondering whether he ought to
take further time off from the search in the library to
go on a probably fruitless errand to see Miss Anstey-

Farthing, when Winston spoke to him on this very matter.

'Look here, Richard,' he said, 'Deborah and I know the old dear – not very well, but well enough to speak to. When Deborah was ill with scarlet fever, she came and brought flowers, and things to eat, and books and such like. She was awfully kind, and she's been a sort of friend to us ever since. I'm sure we could get the book from her if she's got it.'

'Good idea,' said Richard, 'then I can stay here. But you'd better not both go. Couldn't Deborah go alone?'

'I'd better go,' said Winston. 'Then I'd make sure of getting the book. Deborah's a bit vague sometimes.'

'All right – you go. Then Deborah can help go through this stuff. Plenty of it – seems to get more, not less.'

'It's old Jay's copy of *Under the Greenwood Tree* we want, isn't it? Trouble is, she's awfully untidy – I've been in her house two or three times, and it looks as if she rides her motor-bike indoors! You never saw such a mess. It'll probably take a week to find the book.'

'Well, get it if you can,' said Richard, 'and see that she doesn't disturb any loose papers.'

'O.K.,' said Winston. 'I'll go directly after dinner.'

'Come straight back here, won't you – whether you find anything or not.'

As luck would have it, dinner at the Joneses' house was late that day. Mrs Jones, on her way back from the shops, had been waylaid by no less than three acquaintances, who had all wanted to enjoy a lengthy chat on the pavement. So it was not till nearly half past two that Deborah started for the Manor to renew the search, while Winston set off in the opposite direction. He lost no time pedalling through the lower streets of the city, and before long he found himself in the shady windings of Mill Lane.

At the point where the lane crossed a stream, now dried up in the summer drought, a mill house had been erected centuries before. Now, converted into a pleasant modern dwelling, it was inhabited by Miss Anstey-Farthing, her pekinese Mahjong, and her foreign refugee helper and companion.

When Winston arrived, the foreign companion was out, the peke was asleep in a chintz-covered armchair, and Miss Anstey-Farthing poring over an engineering manual. It was she who let Winston in.

'It's Winston Jones,' she said, unnecessarily. 'How glad I am to see you! You must have been sent by Heaven. My bicycle has gone wrong, and I am vainly trying to find out what's the matter. But it's no good. This book tells me nothing. It's all about valves and cam-shafts and Heaven knows what. I shall have to have the man along from the garage – unless you can see what's wrong, that is.'

'Sure,' said Winston obligingly. 'I'll do what I can.'

He hoped he would not have to spend many precious hours tinkering with the motor-cycle, but he could hardly refuse to have anything to do with it.

'But here am I,' went on Miss Anstey-Farthing, 'bothering you with my bothers before you've set foot in the house. What am I thinking of? Do sit down – if you can find somewhere to sit. That's right. How nice to see you! How are your mother and father? And how is your dear sister?'

Winston told her. Then he approached the subject of his visit. The mention of Deborah led easily up to it. He and Richard had agreed, before they parted company before dinner, that Miss Anstey-Farthing had better not be told the truth. Too many people knew of their interest in Mr Jay's possessions already. Perhaps she might gossip – elderly spinsters had been known to do this – and no risks had better be taken. Winston had volunteered to think of a harmless lie.

'As a matter of fact,' he told his hostess, 'I came to find something for Deborah to read.'

'Why, certainly,' agreed Miss Anstey-Farthing. 'As you see, I've lots of books, and I haven't time to read half of them myself. I'd love to lend her something. Would you just like to look round, or is there anything special she wants?'

Winston hesitated. If he said he just wanted to look round, it might take all the afternoon to find the right book; if he mentioned its title, he might be offered the wrong copy, or he might be told it was unsuitable for a girl of thirteen. (Winston had not the remotest idea what the book was about.) On the other hand, if she knew where the book was, it would save a lot of precious time; and if she was certain she had no copy of it, she would tell him straight off, and that too would save time. He decided on a somewhat indirect approach.

'Well, she wondered if you had anything by Thomas Hardy,' he ventured. 'I think they were talking about him at school or something.'

'Really?' said Miss Anstey-Farthing. 'They must have rather adult tastes in literature at Deborah's school. However, I dare say I can find something by Hardy.'

'She said something about one called – er – *Under the Greenwood Tree*, I think it was,' Winston said craftily. 'I hope you don't think *that*'s too difficult. Deborah reads awfully grown-up books sometimes.'

'That's the very one I was going to suggest! A delightful book – I'm sure Deborah would enjoy it.'

This was a huge relief to Winston.

'Let's see if we can find it,' went on Miss Anstey-Farthing. 'You start over there, and I'll look through this lot.'

She was a comfortably built yet remarkably active old lady, and popped about from shelf to shelf talking as she did so.

'You know,' she said, 'I'm sure I had a copy from Mr Jacobus *quite* recently. I often drop into his shop for one thing and another. Such a dear old gentleman, and so very knowing about antiques and curios of all sorts. I got that copper coal-scuttle from him nearly ten years ago. It's a beauty, isn't it? And horse-brasses too – he's ever so good on horse-brasses. I don't care for them myself, but they make excellent presents.'

'I suppose they do,' said Winston doubtfully, 'for people with horses.'

Miss Anstey-Farthing giggled.

'Oh, isn't that delicious!' she said. 'Why, my dear boy, people don't use them for horses any more – they're purely ornamental, you know. They hang them up – like warming-pans and – and – now, what are we looking for? I say, here's an old copy of *The Cuckoo Clock* by Mrs Molesworth. I had it goodness knows how many years ago! I didn't know it was still here. You don't think Deborah would rather have that?'

'I think she's read it,' ventured Winston, who felt he was getting into deep waters. 'I'd rather find *Under the Greenwood Tree*, now that we've started looking for it.'

'Yes, to be sure. Now where *did* I put it? I remember, I was terribly busy at the time I bought it, and I put it away without opening it.'

This at least was good news. But where *had* she put it?

At last Miss Anstey-Farthing gave a high, bird-like cry and darted with surprising quickness to a cupboard in one corner of the room, on top of which there was a row of books supported by a pair of book-ends in the form of squatting elephants.

'Here we are!' she said triumphantly. 'I *knew* I should find it somewhere if we only looked long enough. *Under the Greenwood Tree* by Thomas Hardy.'

She opened the book at the fly-leaf, while Winston hurried across the room to her, if possible, to prevent her from looking through it too thoroughly. If by some miracle the will was inside it, it would be better if she did not find it, as this would mean a long and difficult explanation.

But she was perusing the fly-leaf.

'Why, I see it belonged to old Mr Jay – you know, Mr Jay of Mulbridge Manor, who died only last winter.'

'May I look?' asked Winston. 'Is that his signature?'

This gave him an excuse for taking the book from Miss Anstey-Farthing without appearing too rude.

'Yes, indeed,' she said, letting him have the book.

Winston read the neat, spidery, yet scholarly signature: 'Stephen B. Jay', followed by a date. The elusive volume was found at last.

'Can I borrow it, then?' asked Winston. 'Deborah won't keep it long. She reads terrifically fast.'

'By all means! Keep it as long as you like. And now, I *do* wish you'd just have a glance at my poor little bicycle. Can you spare the time? You boys are so clever with machinery nowadays.'

Winston could scarcely refuse, though he longed for nothing so much as to get the precious book to himself and search through its pages. He dared not do so at the moment, in case the discovery of the will should provoke questions.

'Wait here a moment,' said Miss Anstey-Farthing, 'while I get the key of the shed from the kitchen. I always lock up, you know. This is a lonely spot, and there seem to be so many tramps about nowadays.'

She waddled rapidly off towards the kitchen, and this gave Winston his longed-for opportunity.

Almost dropping the book in his excitement, he turned the pages with trembling fingers. They contained nothing – absolutely nothing except the printed words composed by the novelist. He looked again, but there was not so much as a scrap of loose paper. It was a disappointment, though he and Richard had agreed that there was only a very slender chance that the will would turn up in this way. Oh well, Winston thought, shrugging his shoulders and stuffing the book in the pocket of his blazer, there was nothing for it but to get away as soon as he decently could and report failure to the others.

Much to his surprise, Winston was able to put his hostess's motor-cycle right without much difficulty. He had, as his father was often proud to relate, 'a way with machines'. In this case the trouble was not hard to put right, though it took time, and meant having a good wash afterwards. For a thin copper tube which conveyed petrol from the tank to the carburettor had become blocked with dust; it had first to be disconnected, then freed from obstruction, and finally screwed into place again. They tried starting the motor and a loud, regular popping noise proclaimed the

success of Winston's efforts. Miss Anstey-Farthing was ecstatic in her gratitude and offered Winston tea, which he had much difficulty in refusing. However, after a wash and brush-up, he succeeded in extricating himself from her hospitality, and was once more on his own cycle pedalling hard towards the city, while Miss Anstey-Farthing waved him good-bye from her gate.

If only, Winston reflected, he had been as clever with the search for the will as he had been with the hospitable old lady's ridiculous motor-cycle. What a waste of time! Still, it was nice to have done her a good turn. Meanwhile, he had better get back to the Manor as quickly as he could with the useless volume in his pocket.

So deep in his thoughts was the boy that he failed to notice a strangely assorted pair who strode into the lane from a side-turning at the precise moment when he was passing it. One of the men was lean and stringy, the other somewhat squat in figure; but he had no time to notice this, as he instinctively swerved to avoid them. He was too late. The stringy man walked straight into Winston's cycle, knocked him off it, and clutched at him to save himself from falling. The squat man somehow became involved in the mêlée, and all three, as well as the bicycle, rolled across the lane into a dry ditch on the other side. They disentangled themselves as best they could, while the stringy man groaned and the other cursed.

'Why can't you look where you're going?' he growled. 'Coming round the bend at that speed! Lucky you didn't break your neck, you are!'

The squat man was the first to get himself out of the ditch. Winston was considerably shaken, and the stringy man was groaning, apparently in pain. His seedy grey trousers were torn at the knee, and he was clutching one of his legs with both hands.

'Young devil!' he said. 'What the blazes are you doing?'

But Winston was too sorry for himself to answer. His face was cut, the pocket of his blazer was almost torn off, and his bicycle was twisted. He picked it out of the ditch, and then gave his attention to the groaning man. The other was nowhere to be seen. For some reason he had disappeared from view, leaving his companion to suffer alone. After a few moments the stringy man calmed down and asked Winston how he felt.

'I'm O.K.,' said Winston. 'I'm sorry I ran into you. I didn't see you – honestly I didn't.'

'You couldn't help it, I guess,' said the man grudgingly. 'Only you want to be more careful. I'd better get going and see what's become of my mate.'

'Are you sure you can walk?' asked Winston.

'Yeah,' said the man. 'I'll manage. You all right?'

'I think so,' said Winston. 'I'm sorry if it was my fault.'

'Can't be helped now,' said the man. 'So long.'

And for one who had only just been groaning with pain, he made off at considerable speed.

Winston adjusted his saddle and handlebars as best he could and was about to remount when he realized that the book he had just borrowed was no longer in his pocket. He got down once more into the ditch and searched in the long grass. It was not there. Nor was it in the hedge which overhung the ditch. The boy even looked through the hedge into the field on the other side, but there was no sign of the missing book. After an unsuccessful search of the whole scene of the accident, Winston concluded that one of the men must have made off with it. What a rum thing to do! Should he go back to Mill House and explain to the owner that he had apparently been robbed of her book? Better to get on his cycle again and see if he could catch the two men. He could at least ask them if they had seen it.

He made as good speed as he could in view of his bruises and the shaky condition of his cycle, but he failed to overtake the two men. They must have taken one of the several side lanes that turned off into the meadowland on either side of the road.

So that was that, it seemed. He wondered whether to go home and tidy up, but he shrank from the explanations and the delay that this would mean. He decided to get back to Mulbridge Manor as quickly as he could.

He wanted to find out how the search had been going in the library; he wanted food and drink – if there was any left; but above all, he wanted to tell the others the story of his strange accident.

Was he so sure it *was* an accident? It looked very much as if the two gentlemen in Mill Lane had deliberately knocked him off his bicycle in order to see what he had in his pockets. Yes, that was it! It was they who had overturned the headquarters in the barn and taken Richard's journal. This had told them about the lost copy of *Under the Greenwood Tree* and given them the idea of spying on any of the children who might be trying to get it back. But who were they, and what did they want the will for? Were they the two whom Richard had named 'Seedy' and 'Dusty'? Certainly they had answered the description.

Busy with these thoughts, Winston cycled past the cathedral just as the great clock was striking five. If he was to get any tea, he had better hurry. He pedalled harder; but now, turning into the road that would lead up to the heath, he cycled with extreme care, looking this way and that. He was not going to be knocked off his bicycle twice by any unseen desperadoes!

Chapter Eleven

MR GERALD JAY AT HOME

THE two gentlemen who had knocked Winston off his bicycle and stolen the unoffending Miss Anstey-Farthing's copy of *Under the Greenwood Tree* were no longer at large among the lanes about Mulcaster. They had just boarded the evening train for London. Having assured themselves that the book contained nothing of interest, they had disgustedly pitched it over a hedge into the nearest meadow. They had returned as rapidly as possible to their lodgings at a small commercial hotel in Mulcaster, made themselves as presentable as nature would allow, and caught the train by the skin of their teeth.

In the train they said little, although they had the carriage to themselves. The gentleman whom we have christened 'Dusty' contented himself with smoking cigarettes and reading the sporting columns of an evening paper. His companion, 'Seedy', took from his case a certain exercise book and re-read it thoughtfully. Then shrugging his shoulders, he put it away again and settled down to await the announcement of dinner.

The two men dined as expensively as the British Railways allow and treated themselves to drinks and cigars in a manner which suggested they were not paying for their own entertainment.

An hour or so later, Mr Gerald Jay, the very gentleman who was in fact paying their expenses, was impatiently awaiting their arrival at his London flat. It was luxuriously furnished in the taste of an expensive decorator. Gerald was expensively dressed. Everything suggested that it would have hurt him considerably to have to do without money – money in large and constant supply.

The train from Mulcaster was late, so that it was a more than usually impatient Gerald who at last opened the door to his two guests. Their shabbiness contrasted strikingly with their employer's natty appearance. Gerald was tall; his well-shaved face was handsome, and his manner was that of one who can afford to order others about. Nevertheless, the two men did not dislike him. Perhaps they were used to being ordered about; and certainly their employer was not mean.

'So you've shown up at last,' said Gerald sarcastically, as he closed the door behind them. 'Very good of you, I'm sure.'

'Couldn't be helped,' said Seedy. 'Ran for the train, we did – and then it was late in.'

'I've been waiting all day. I told you to come and report this morning.'

'Couldn't get away,' volunteered Dusty. 'Somethink important happened.'

'Don't tell me you've got what I want?' said Gerald.

'No, we ain't,' answered Dusty. 'Nor 'as anybody else neither, not yet.'

'I see. Well, come and sit down and tell me all about it.'

The two men sank themselves and their disreputable

clothes into Gerald's immaculate armchairs. They stretched out their legs luxuriously and looked as if they would like some refreshment.

'Warm evening, Mr Jay,' said Seedy.

'It is,' agreed Gerald. 'Like the window open?'

'I've had plenty of fresh air this last week.'

'Then perhaps you'd like a drink?'

Seedy said nothing. Gerald poured out three drinks, placed cigars at his guests' elbows, and all three made themselves comfortable.

'Gentlemen,' said Gerald after some minutes. 'You don't look happy. I've given you some of my whisky and a couple of my best – well, let's say my second best – cigars, but you still don't look happy. Are you short of money?'

'We'll come to that later. I know you won't stint us, Mr Jay, but it's not that.'

'No? Well, what is it?'

'Fact is,' said Dusty, 'we don't like the job. We don't know what we're looking for – leastways, we don't know if there *is* such a thing at all.'

'Perhaps there isn't,' said Gerald. 'In that case, we shall all be happy. You'll get your fee, and I'll get my house.'

'It would be a sight easier if it wasn't for all them kids running round,' pursued Dusty. 'If there's one thing I can't stand mixed up in a job, it's kids. Nearly hurt one of them this afternoon, we did. Looks bad, you know – hurting a kid – if anything should come out.'

'Don't tell me you've been clumsy,' said Gerald. 'Surely the man that got away with the Liverpool mail-bag robbery last year, the man the police are still look-ing for, isn't going to be put off by a few school-children?'

'You don't have to bring that up,' said Dusty angrily.

'Oh, but I think of it constantly,' said Gerald. 'It reminds me how skilful you are – and how much I know about you, just in case anything should go wrong.'

'There's plenty we know about you too, Mr Jay,' put in Seedy, 'if it comes to that.'

'Now we mustn't begin by quarrelling,' said Gerald. 'So far everything is splendid. You haven't found the will, but nor has anyone else. What could be better? A couple of days ago I got my lawyer to write to the old lady another letter threatening to turn her out if she can't produce a will pretty quickly. I fancy they'll give up trying soon. But how do you know they haven't found it?'

'Take a look at this,' said Seedy, handing his employer the exercise book containing Richard's private journal. Gerald studied the page carefully, and Dusty, taking advantage of their host's abstraction, poured out more drinks.

'What's this?' asked Gerald at last. 'It reminds me of when I used to play detectives at school.'

'Just what these kids are doing,' answered Seedy. 'There's six of them. They're ransacking every book in the old man's library in case he stuck his will in one of them before he died. It seems one of them got the idea it might be in this – what's it? – *Under the Green Tree*, or whatever it is, on account of something the old man said before he died, I guess. Kind of crazy, if you ask me, but we can't afford to –'

'Leave a stone unturned, you were going to say,' suggested Gerald.

'That's right. We followed one of the kids all the way to some daft old girl's house at the back of beyond this afternoon. Staged a slight accident – no bones broken, you understand – and pinched the book off him. I had a good look through his pockets too, while we were rolling in the ditch. But there was nothing on him, I'll swear to that.'

'Was it wise to – er – remove this notebook from wherever you found it?' asked Gerald. 'Surely you must have aroused the young detectives' suspicions by now?'

'Couldn't do nothing else,' said Dusty. 'Too much of it to copy in the middle of the night with only a pocket torch. They *may* suspect, but it don't make no difference. The kid we pushed off his bike this afternoon hadn't seen us before. For all he knows, it was pure accident.'

'I should think he'd have a fair idea about that,' said Seedy.

'What's to prevent their going to the police and getting them to take over the business? That's what'll happen if you use any more violence.'

'We didn't hurt him, I tell you,' said Seedy. 'We saw him ride off on his bike afterwards, fit as –'

'A fiddle, no doubt.'

'Fit as anything. They might go to the police, but I don't think so. Firstly, they've got nothing to *take* to the police. Secondly, kids don't like the police, and the police don't like kids. Thirdly, they want to solve the thing themselves – that's child-psychology. Turning it over to the police would be like losing a cricket match to them. Fifthly –'

'Fourthly, I think you mean.'

'O.K., smarty – fourthly, the local police are a pretty sleepy lot – only crime they've ever had round there was when somebody poisoned the vicar's prize vegetable marrow the week before the flower show. Fifthly, the old dame – begging your pardon, Mr Jay, your dear old auntie would never go to the police. They know her. Nobody thinks there's a will at all. They think the old dear is cuckoo. So she is – begging your pardon.'

Gerald laughed.

'Yes, indeed, my poor old Aunt Matty. What a character! All the same, she's a nuisance. What on earth does she want a place like that for? It's mine, I tell you – mine by rights, and if that old girl stands in my way, I'll strangle her with her own bead necklace.'

'She don't want it for 'erself,' said Dusty. 'She wants to give it away for a hospital or something.'

'She *would*,' said Gerald savagely. 'Sentimental old ditherer. What's needed down there is a nice select country club. I've got plans, I tell you. There's a bit of land around the house, and if it's to be bought, we can turn it into a golf club, or maybe a race track. There's money there – and jobs for you boys, if you're interested.'

Gerald filled their glasses up and handed out two more of his second-best cigars, as if to remind them how generous he could be when he liked.

'Have you seen my respected aunt?' he went on.

'Yeah,' said Dusty. 'She's moved out of the Manor –'

'Has she, though?' asked Gerald thoughtfully. 'That shows she's crazy. Makes it easier for me to get in, don't you see. But go on.'

'She hasn't moved altogether,' said Seedy. 'She's living at a sort of crummy hotel called "Rosebank" in the next village, and she goes up to the Manor every day and hangs around.'

'Why didn't you move into this hotel yourselves? You could have kept an eye on her.'

'*She* could have kept an eye on *us* too,' said Seedy. 'We're not the sort that stays there. It's mostly retired school-teachers and parsons on fishing holidays. Very select, you know. Too genteel for us.'

'She's got a dog,' said Dusty. 'Harmless enough – half-blind, I should think. But it gives her a bit of trouble in this "Rosebank" dump.'

'She's got a horse too,' said Seedy.

'Don't tell me Aunty Matty rides?' said Gerald. 'I wouldn't be surprised, mind you. She'd do anything.'

'No – it's just a retired hack she keeps in the paddock. I tried to buy it.'

'Whatever for?' asked Gerald. 'You're not going to challenge the Aga Khan at the next Derby, are you?'

'No, but I thought I might get into the house and have a talk with the old – with your aunt.'

'Have you been inside?'

'No. Didn't want to show ourselves too much. While the kids are busy finding the will, why should we bother?'

'True. But with your unique experience, I should have thought you might assist the search by lending a hand yourselves.'

'O.K., we'll have a look round one of these shiny nights, if we have to. But we don't want to do anything to get the authorities interested in us, if we can help it.'

Gerald splashed some more whisky into his guests' glasses.

'Well,' he said, 'keep on as you are. I should think another week would see it through – a couple of weeks at most. After that, if my solicitor can't frighten the old lady into giving up the property, he'll have to serve her a court order to get out.'

'And if the will turns up?' asked Seedy, eyeing his employer keenly over the rim of his glass.

'Get it,' said Gerald, his mouth for a moment suggesting the appearance of a rat-trap. 'Get it anyhow you like. If you get yourselves into trouble, that's your affair. But if you bring it to me, safe and sound, you know your fee. You can trust me – as I trust you. The moment you get it, bring it to me. If the Manor's left to my aunt, we can tear the will up there and then, and she'll never get it. You'll have your share – don't worry about that.'

'We trust you, Mr Jay,' said Dusty. 'When 'ave we said we don't?'

'If the authorities are nosing around, and it isn't safe for you to have the will on you till you can reach me, don't hesitate to destroy it. But destroy it properly, mind you. No leaving pieces about in hotel wastepaper baskets. Burn it, if necessary.'

'How'll you know we've burnt it?' asked Seedy, again looking sharply at Gerald. 'Perhaps you'll say we never got it at all and you're not going to pay us our money.'

'You mustn't be so suspicious,' said Gerald genially. 'We must all trust each other. You'll be each other's witnesses. I can afford to pay you what I've promised. Why should I double-cross you? If you tell me you've destroyed the will and you haven't, I shall know soon enough. My aunt's solicitor will have it filed, and my solicitor will know straight away. If you're thinking of double-crossing *me* by any chance, you won't get away with it. If you tell me you've destroyed the will and you haven't, either there never *was* one, which will suit me just as well, or my aunt's lawyer will produce it. In the first case you'll get your money, in the second case you won't. So why not let's all trust each other?'

Gerald got up, went across to his desk, and unlocked a drawer.

'Here,' he said. 'You'll be needing more cash. Twenty-five each a week, I think we said, until it's all over. Here's a couple of weeks' expenses in advance, just to show I trust you.'

He handed each of his guests a reassuringly fat

packet of bank-notes. They took them in silence, and each placed his packet in his breast pocket with scarcely more than a glance at it.

'Aren't you going to count it?' asked Gerald, with a note of mockery in his voice.

'You know us, Mr Jay,' said Seedy, 'and we know you. I guess we can trust each other.'

'I guess so,' said Gerald pleasantly, showing his teeth in a smile. 'Does that go for you too?'

'Sure,' said Dusty.

'You'll be needing some sleep if you're to be back on the job first thing. First train in the morning, mind.'

'Six o'clock sharp at Waterloo,' said Dusty.

'Good,' said Gerald.

The two men got up.

'One for the road?' asked their host, indicating the whisky decanter.

'Don't mind if I do,' said Dusty.

Gerald poured out a generous stirrup-cup, which the two men drained in a silent and business-like manner. Then they took their leave and went.

Gerald went to the window and watched them as they emerged from the building. Before going to bed, he was devoutly thanking his good fortune that it was they, and not he, who had to be at Waterloo station at six in the morning. He was a man accustomed to having his own way, and paying for it.

Chapter Twelve

ANXIETY AT 'ROSEBANK'

MISS MATILDA JAY was not finding life easy at 'Rosebank'. True, her friend Mrs Mosscrop was kindness itself, and Ivy the maid did her best to make the newcomer comfortable. But it is not the same as having one's own home. She would not have minded the daily tramp up the dusty gravel lane to the Manor if only the weather had been cooler. Dennis would pant along beside her; yet on account of the heat, she did not always let him come, so that he had taken to straying.

Indeed, only the other day a policeman from Mulcaster had appeared at the entrance to 'Rosebank' with Dennis on a lead, demanding to see Miss Jay, whose name was on the collar.

'I've been up to the Manor,' he said, 'but I'm told you live here now. One of the farmers over Mulcaster way came and complained of your dog, he did. Said he'd been among his cows, upsetting them like. Interferes with their milk, seemingly, to be worried by dogs in hot weather.'

'Oh dear, oh dear!' sighed Matty. 'I do hope Dennis did no harm. Really, he's a very friendly dog, constable. He wouldn't hurt a fly.'

'The farmer who brought him to me,' continued the police constable severely, 'said as how he was a-going to shoot him if he catches him among his cows again. So I'm warning you, ma'am. That's all.'

'Shoot him!' said Matty, aghast. 'How *could* anyone shoot Dennis? It's not human! It's – it's –'

'Well, that's what he said, ma'am. I'm only warning you. Stray dogs can be a lot of trouble to the police, so I must ask you to look after him better. I don't want to be unreasonable, but it's up to you, for the sake of the dog, as well as other people, to see that he doesn't wander.'

At the conclusion of this brief lecture, the constable handed over Dennis to his mortified owner and departed with dignity.

'Pompous idiot!' said Matty, when the constable was out of earshot. 'How can I look after Dennis properly in a strange house? I can't tie him up all day. The gate's nearly always left open, so of course Dennis can get out.'

The problem was not easily solved. Matty gave the dog a good talking-to, and the dog looked very ashamed, but he did not altogether promise not to stray in the future.

Then there were the other guests at 'Rosebank'. Some of them were very chatty, and never let her alone. Not that she objected to a chat when she felt like it; but she did not always feel like it, and she never seemed able to escape from inquisitive people with too little to do. Just now she was worried, and she did not want to talk to strangers about the weather, and their ailments, and their grandchildren. She was worried about Dennis, but more especially she was worried about her brother's will. Would it ever be found? Even the gallant Matty was beginning to have her doubts. Stephen had told her the Manor was to be hers – of that there was no mistake. But then, Stephen had been so very odd and strange towards the end that perhaps he had only imagined he had made a will in her favour. Perhaps she was giving those dear children all that

trouble for nothing. After all, if the County did not get its hospital, it was not her fault. There were plenty of rich people in the County. Let *them* pay to have one built. Then she thought of her utterly selfish nephew Gerald, with his sarcastic manner and heartless ways, and she almost made up her mind that, sooner than let him have it to turn into a racing club or a smart hotel, she would set fire to the Manor herself and burn it down.

Not all the guests at 'Rosebank' were tiresome. One of them, a certain Doctor Eastwell, who had arrived the day after Matty, was unusually pleasant and genial. Goodness knows what he was a doctor of – certainly not medicine. It was generally supposed, among the regular guests, that he must be a doctor of science. They immediately nicknamed him 'the Professor'. Nobody could find out exactly what he was doing at Mulbridge. Even old Mrs Fitzjohn, who had been to 'Rosebank' every summer for the past fifteen years, and made it her business to find out everything about any newcomer, had been able to discover nothing except that the Professor was there on holiday, that he was a naturalist by profession, and went about collecting butterflies and other insects. He spent much of his time rambling about the countryside, returning in time for meals, sometimes with a butterfly-net and a killing-bottle, sometimes with a camera. He was invariably courteous, interesting, and pleasant to talk to, and never gave away much about himself, even to Mrs Fitzjohn.

He had even been seen climbing about the roof of 'Rosebank' in rubber shoes, peering under ledges and drain-pipes in search of interesting objects, such as a little patch of moss or the chrysalis of a butterfly. Of course he had asked Mrs Mosscrop's permission first.

Matty found him pleasant to talk to. He did not tell her about his sister-in-law's operation or his own winter ailments, nor was he curious about her private affairs. Instead, he talked to her about the flowers and animals of the countryside, and about old legends and sayings he had heard from the mouths of local folk.

After lunch, on the day of Seedy and Dusty's early return from London, he was sitting beside Matty in a shady corner of the lawn behind the house. Not far away, in another deck-chair Mrs Fitzjohn, while pretending to be asleep over her newspaper, was doing her best to overhear their conversation. But even she was obliged to admit to herself that what she heard was of very little interest.

'The birds round here,' the Professor was saying, 'are of quite remarkable interest. Even in this hot weather, when birds in many parts of the country have almost given up singing, they have as fresh and cheerful voices as any blackbird in June.'

'Indeed?' said Matty. 'But they are famous, of course. Everyone has heard of the Mulbridge thrushes.'

'Yes,' agreed the Professor, 'even our friends of the B.B.C. have heard of them, and I believe they are sending someone down to make recordings in the bird sanctuary in Mulbridge Woods.'

Matty looked doubtful.

'I don't know that Mulbridge ought to be broadcast,' she said. 'Publicity doesn't do a place any good, does it?'

'Well, I don't know. The tradesmen and boarding-house keepers don't mind a bit of publicity. It brings customers, you know, and –'

'Goodness me!' Matty interrupted. 'Where's Dennis? I do believe –'

But her fear was unnecessary. Dennis was asleep, curled up beneath Mrs Fitzjohn's deck-chair.

'There he is,' said the Professor, adding under his breath: 'I do hope our good landlady's deck-chairs are well made. The poor fellow seems to be unaware of the danger he is in.'

'Have you been finding anything interesting round here?' Matty asked. 'Any insects and butterflies, and whatever else you collect?'

'Yes, indeed,' said the Professor. 'My note-book is full of curious observations, and I have one or two specimens that will interest my naturalist friends. I wonder,' he went on, 'if there are any unusual creatures about the grounds of the Manor?'

'I dare say,' said Matty. 'Certainly nobody comes there to disturb them, if there are.'

'I should think the Manor would be a wonderful breeding-ground for birds.'

'You can go and have a look any time you like,' said Matty. 'I'm afraid things are very untidy and neglected, but you're welcome to have a look round.'

'Thank you,' said the Professor, 'and if things are rather neglected, so much the better, from a naturalist's point of view. I want to make a nocturnal ramble in search of moths. They are best seen at night – indeed, some of them never appear in the day-time at all. If I took a look among your ancient trees one of these warm, moonlight nights, who knows what I might find?'

'A jolly good idea,' agreed Matty heartily. 'You go up there any night you like. Don't frighten Dragon, that's all. He's an old horse I keep in the paddock, though what we'll do with him when –'

Here she stopped. She was not going to bother the

Professor with her private troubles, and she had no intention of embarking on the full story of the will and her promise of the Manor to the local Medical Committee if she should ever come into possession of it.

Just then Ivy appeared in the garden to tell Miss Matilda that some of the children had called to see her. Should she send them into the garden?

'Yes, please, Ivy,' said Matty, who was too comfortable to get up at that moment unless she absolutely had to – 'that is, if you don't mind?' she added, turning to the Professor.

'Not at all, not at all,' said he. 'Receive your visitors out here by all means. As a matter of fact, I have to go in and write some letters, so they won't disturb me.'

The children had spent the morning going through most of the remaining books in the library. After their fruitless search they had returned to their homes late for lunch. Afterwards Richard and Cherry had called for Winston and Deborah as usual, and they had all agreed to go by way of Mulbridge and make a call on Matty. As they approached 'Rosebank' they were greeted by a familiar figure. It was Seedy.

'Hullo,' he called. 'Warm day again! Did you think to ask the old lady at the Manor if she wants to sell her horse?'

'She doesn't want to sell him,' answered Richard, putting his foot to the ground and balancing his bicycle with Cherry perched on the carrier. Then the man recognized Winston, who had also stopped at the sight of him.

'Why, good day, young fellow. You and I have met before – only yesterday, wasn't it? Any damage done to the cycle?'

'No,' said Winston. 'But I'd like to know what happened to my book.'

'Book?' asked Seedy, with a puzzled air. 'What book?'

'I was carrying a book in my pocket when you ran into me. I thought perhaps you might have seen it.'

'I didn't see any book. Wouldn't have any use for it if I did! I expect you dropped it in the ditch.'

'I looked there,' said Winston.

'Well, you ought to be thankful you're not hurt yourself – dashing round the bend like that! Ah well, I must be getting along. Glad to have seen you. If the old lady changes her mind about that horse, just you let me know. Call at The Grapes down in Mulcaster, and they'll know where to find me. So long.'

He sauntered off in the direction of Mulcaster, and the children went on to 'Rosebank'. In two minutes' time they were being shown into the pleasant, shady garden by the maid Ivy.

Matty introduced them to the Professor, who spoke politely to each of them in turn, and then answered a number of questions they put to him about natural history and the care of pets. He answered patiently and helpfully and then excused himself on the ground that he had letters to write. They had been delighted to talk to such a charming and well-informed man.

'We were wondering if you were going up to the Manor this afternoon,' said Richard. 'We could walk up with you.'

'I wasn't thinking of going today,' said Matty, 'but if there's anything special, I could go. The fact is, I'm rather upset. Dennis has been straying again. I don't seem able to turn my head without him wandering off. I suppose it's the move that has made him restless.'

'Never mind, if you don't want to come,' said Richard. 'Is there anywhere we could talk?'

He lowered his voice, having noted the presence of Mrs Fitzjohn and one or two other guests not far away.

'I tell you what,' said Matty. 'I'll stroll a little of the way with you. It'll give Dennis a bit of exercise.'

On hearing his name, the elderly retriever pricked up his ears, crept out from under the form of Mrs Fitzjohn, and stood beside his mistress expectantly.

'What about a teeny-weeny stroll, Dennis?' suggested Matty.

Dennis readily agreed, and they set out, the children wheeling their bicycles.

'I can tell by your expressions,' said Matty as soon as they were clear of 'Rosebank', 'that you didn't have any luck this morning.'

'No,' said Winston. 'We're nearly at the end of the books now. Honestly, Miss Jay, I don't think there's a chance of finding it. P'raps there wasn't a will at all. But more likely, we've been barking up the wrong tree all the time. Wish we could think of somewhere else to look, but it seems pretty hopeless.'

'The wrong tree,' repeated Matty, absently, 'barking up the wrong tree. I suppose we'll have to admit failure. It *does* seem a shame.'

She looked very woebegone.

'My brother never meant this to happen, you know. There's an awful mistake somewhere. I feel sure there is.'

'We are wondering, Miss Jay,' began Richard.

'Yes?' said Matty.

'We were wondering if you'd mind if we had a moonlight feast at H.Q. – the paddock barn, you know. It would be such fun. It's full moon tonight.'

'What would your parents say?' asked Matty.

'Our parents don't mind – for once,' said Deborah, 'as it's holidays.'

'My parents are away,' said Richard. 'They've taken a few days off to go to the Norfolk Broads. Some friends of ours have got a boat. There's only room for Mummy and Daddy – worse luck. Not that we'd have gone, and left you in the lurch – would we, Cherry?'

'No fear,' said Cherry. 'What's the lurch, Richard?'

'Something you don't leave people in,' answered her brother. 'Our Aunt Frances is looking after us while they're away. She's Mummy's sister. She's a sport; she won't mind us being out at night, just this once, as we'll be with others. Oh, do say yes, Miss Jay! We might get a new idea – a real brainwave.'

'Fat lot of good your brainwaves are,' said Winston. 'Last time your brain waved, I got knocked off my bike.'

'Shut up,' said Richard. 'What do you say, Miss Jay?'

'Well, of course, if your parents really have no objection, I wouldn't dream of stopping you.'

'Oh, thank you, Miss Jay!' they all said excitedly. 'It'll be super! We won't be too late.'

'And I'll tell you what,' Matty continued. 'I'll give you five shillings for some cakes and ginger-pop, or whatever you children drink nowadays. When I was a girl, it was always ginger-pop.'

'Hooray!' said Winston. 'Three cheers for Miss Jay.'

'No, please,' said Matty. 'You'll terrify Dennis. Here's the five shillings, and mind you don't set fire to the barn, or break your necks, or anything dreadful.'

'No fear. Don't worry, Miss Jay. Thanks awfully for the five bob. It's tremendously good of you.'

'And you *will* have a last search tomorrow, won't you?' pleaded Matty.

To this they agreed with alacrity. So Matty returned to 'Rosebank', talking to Dennis about nothing in particular, and the others went off to tell Beaver and Anne about the moonlight feast.

That feast was one of the most memorable in the children's history. Aunt Frances even allowed Cherry to go, so great was her faith in Richard. Matty's five shillings, together with other lesser sums they were able to raise, purchased an astonishing number of vivid and dangerous-looking cakes, and a sufficient quantity of fizzy drink to launch a battleship. As soon as darkness had fallen and the moon was full, they met Beaver and proceeded to the village to call for Anne. Mr and Mrs Shipley did not like the idea of Anne's going out at that time of night, but what could they do against the eloquent pleading of the five other children? It was a wonderful night, warm and still; there was no need to get up early next day; Mrs Shipley now had her husband at home to see to her needs, and altogether Anne would be missing the chance of a lifetime if she were not allowed to go.

In the barn everything was dark and eerie, except where the brilliant white moonlight flooded in through the open door and the window. It was the same H.Q. as ever, but how different in the August moonlight!

The cakes were spread out, the bottles opened, and the feast began. For all the novelty and the excitement of the occasion, it had about it almost an air of sadness. They had failed in their search. Only a few books were left to give up their secrets, and little hope remained.

So it behoved everyone to think hard, to discover some new source of inspiration. The will *must* be somewhere. If only they thought hard enough. . . .

There was silence except for the hooting of an owl and the gentle sound of Dragon cropping the long grass away in a far corner of the paddock. At last the boys wandered off to talk in broken murmurs at the back of the barn. Anne and Cherry began to gather up the bottles and other remains of the spread. Deborah, her mind full – but full of what, she could not say – found herself straying across the paddock towards the dark bulk of the old horse. She was going to do something she had longed to do for days, but had not quite dared – she could not tell why.

She came up quite close to Dragon. The horse took no notice. He knew her well.

'Dragon, old fellow,' she said quietly, 'may I? May I have a ride – just a little one? Do say yes.'

She put her arms round his neck as he turned his head to stare at her. He did not seem to mind. Somehow she managed to scramble on to his back, and there she sat, as proud as if she had been a princess mounted high on some delicate Arab steed. She clicked her tongue twice, and Dragon began slowly to wander about the paddock, stopping now and again to crop a mouthful of grass, sweetly scented in the warm night air.

The horse moved slowly towards a dark patch of trees. The branches grew so thick, and the leaves were so broad that scarcely any moonlight pierced them, and the ground beneath was a deep velvety black.

Dragon took half-a-dozen paces into the gloom, then stopped. All at once he shied, whinnied violently and turned, breaking into a canter, while Deborah clung tightly round his neck. The noise of the whinnying, hideous and terrifying in the still night air, brought the other children out of the barn.

'What's that?' ejaculated Richard.

'Deborah,' shouted Winston, 'where are you?'

Beyond the scared horse who now showed huge in the moonlight, they saw, or thought they saw, a faint glow in the darkness. It moved swiftly and then went out. At the same time they heard clearly the sound of feet swishing through the grass. There was a muffled clink as something fell to the ground. Then for a few seconds, silhouetted against the grey, moonlit wall of part of the Manor, they saw the figure of a man. Almost instantly, he was out of sight.

'Come on!' said Beaver, taking the lead for once. 'Let's see what he's up to.'

Richard and he ran swiftly across the grass to where the man had disappeared, while Winston remained behind to see that his sister was unhurt and the two other girls were not frightened.

'You all right, Deborah?' he said, as the horse came to a standstill beside him, and Deborah slipped to the ground.

'I'm all right,' she said. 'He *saw* somebody, Winston – there was somebody under the trees, I think, going round with a torch. Who *could* it have been?'

At that moment Richard and Beaver reappeared round the corner of the house. The others went to meet them.

'See anyone?' asked Winston.

'Not a soul. Whoever it was has vamoosed. Hullo, what's this?'

Something lying in the grass caught Richard's eye as it gleamed in the moonlight. He stopped and picked up a glass bottle. It must have been what the man had dropped as he switched off his torch and bolted. The muffled clink they heard had been made by the bottle hitting a stone buried in the grass. Richard held it up for them all to see. It was no ordinary bottle. It was short and squat, with a wide neck, into which a wooden-topped cork stopper was tightly fitted. Inside the bottle was a white solid substance – and three or four dead moths.

'Why, it's a killing-bottle!' Richard said in sudden recognition. 'Who on earth could have been carrying that?'

The question remained, for the time being, un-answered, for just then Cherry began to cry.

'I want to go home,' she moaned.

The excitement of the moonlight feast and the un-expected adventure which had followed it had suddenly become too much for her. After a hasty conference, it was decided that there was nothing further to be done at that hour. It was time they started for home. Richard picked up his sister and carried her back to the barn, where they lost no time in lighting their cycle lamps and starting for home.

Chapter Thirteen

DEBORAH HAS A DREAM

AUNT FRANCES wisely did not expect Richard and Cherry to get up early. The sun was already high in the sky, and the mid-August day unusually hot when they left home to meet the others for the final attack on the library. Late as it was, there were by now only sufficient books left to occupy them for the rest of the morning.

The Joneses were waiting for them, and outside the Manor they met Beaver and Anne.

All six children showed signs of having been up late the night before; but everyone had an air of cheerfulness – an almost forced air, you might have said. It was the last day of the search; perhaps success would reward their efforts on this very last morning; but whatever happened, they knew they had done their best.

After they had stacked their cycles inside headquarters, they had a brief discussion. What was to be done about the intruder of the night before?

Undoubtedly someone had been lurking in the paddock with a torch, and had taken fright at the appearance of the moonlight banqueters. Obviously that someone was the Professor, to whom they had been introduced the previous day at 'Rosebank'. What was he doing at the Manor?

'He was on a moonlight bug-hunt,' said Winston. 'Snooping around with a torch to attract moths. Caught some too, but not very exciting ones.'

They had a look inside the killing-bottle and found that the Professor's specimens were nothing out of the ordinary.

'Yes, that's about it,' said Deborah. 'I expect he had Matty's permission. She seemed to be very friendly with him.'

'That's right,' said Beaver.

'Well then, let's get on with the last lot of books,' said Anne.

'Half a minute,' said Richard. 'There's just one thing that's puzzling me. If he was just snooping round for moths, and had Matty's permission to be in the paddock at night, why did he do a bunk like that as soon as he saw us? That's what I want to know.'

Nobody spoke. At last Winston said slowly:

'Something in that, you know. He left in a hurry. Didn't even stop to pick up his bottle.'

'That's a very brainy notion,' said Beaver. 'What do you think yourself, Richard?'

'I haven't an idea,' said Richard. 'Perhaps he thought we were somebody else.'

'Perhaps he had no right to be there at all,' said Deborah.

'Well, come on,' said Anne, 'it's no good wasting time talking about it.'

'Look here,' said Richard. 'I vote we don't bother about it any more at present, but just tell Matty next time we see her. Obviously she didn't know he was going to be there, or she'd have warned us. But she may know *something* about it.'

This was generally agreed to, and, taking out of his pocket the key to the french window which Matty had lent them, Richard led the way to the library.

'Hullo,' he said, 'the door's unlocked.'

'Perhaps Matty's here,' suggested someone.

But not only was Matty not at the Manor, it was obvious that someone else had been there during the night. For many of the books had been pulled out of the shelves at random and left on the floor, on chairs, or anywhere else that was handy, and the neat piles of paper which had been left on the centre table – bills in one pile, letters in another, circulars in another, and so on – these had been scattered here and there in the utmost disorder.

One thing, however, they were all quick to notice. The stack of shelves which still remained to be searched had been left untouched by the intruder or intruders.

'What are we going to do about this?' asked Winston, when they had taken stock of the disorder.

'Perhaps we ought to have the police in,' Richard said. 'It's obvious some outsider really has been trespassing. Must have had a skeleton key too – or picked the lock. It's a bad business. Have a look round, everyone, and see if they've left any clues.'

While the rest searched the library for clues, Richard had a quick glance round the rest of the house. But outside the library there was no sign whatever of any intrusion. Nor was anything found in the library itself which could possibly be called a clue.

'If this was in a book,' said Richard sadly, 'there'd be at least a trousers button or a cigarette end.'

There was certainly nothing so helpful to be found amidst the disorder on the floor, the chairs, and the tables.

'I suppose the Professor was having a look round,' said Deborah. 'What a pity! He seemed such a nice man.'

'Well, are you going to call the cops?' Winston asked Richard.

'No,' answered Richard, 'I think I'd better tell Matty first. It's a bit awkward, because if we tell the police, they'll want to know the whole story; then they'll wonder why Matty didn't go to them in the first place. Besides, it isn't as if whoever it was has broken anything or stolen anything – so far as we can see.'

'Somebody pinched your journal the other night,' said Beaver.

'Yeah,' said Winston, 'and that Seedy chap knew more than he let on about that book I was carrying the other day when he conveniently knocked me off my bike.'

'The whole thing is getting very fishy,' agreed Richard, 'but I vote we finish the search first. Suppose I go down to see if Matty's in, while you others get on with this lot of books. Anybody want to come with me?'

'Let me come, Richard,' said Cherry.

'I'll come, if you want a bodyguard,' volunteered Beaver.

'I'd love to come,' said Anne.

It was decided that Anne should accompany Richard to 'Rosebank', as she had not been there before. Together they set off across the heath and down the gravelled road leading to the village.

Poor Matty, when she learned that they wanted to speak to her privately, hoped they had brought the will with them. Overcoming her disappointment, she listened to their story, and then said:

'I can explain why the Professor was there, anyway. He told me yesterday that he would like to look for moths in the Manor grounds some moonlight night, and I told him he might. I must say, I didn't expect he would be there last night, otherwise I would have warned you.'

'Yes,' said Richard. 'But why did he disappear so quickly? That's what we want to know.'

'Well, that I can't say,' said Matty. 'Naturalists are funny people, you know. I expect they prefer to move in a mysterious way. I know him quite well, and I'm sure there's nothing wrong with him.'

'How do you know?' persisted Richard. 'You haven't known him long. He may be your nephew in disguise, for all you can tell.'

Matty laughed.

'Oh no,' she said. 'I know Gerald too well for that. But if you like, I can ask him what he was doing last night.'

'I shouldn't do that *yet*,' said Richard. 'Give us a chance to finish the job. But you could return his killing-bottle, if you like, and see if he says anything. Just say it was found in the paddock this morning.'

'All right,' agreed Matty, taking the bottle, which Richard fished out of his pocket and handed to her. 'It won't kill *me*, I hope.'

'Not unless you get inside it,' said Richard.

As to the other matter – the nocturnal trespass in the

library – it was agreed to wait a little before reporting
that to the police. After the affair of Dennis and the
angry farmer, Matty had no wish to trouble the Mulcaster constabulary unnecessarily. But she must not
delay long, since the police would certainly want to
know why the matter had not been reported instantly;
so it was decided that she would tell the police about
the intruder as soon as the children had given up the
search for the will.

'But you won't give up, will you?' Matty appealed.
'Not till there's absolutely no hope.'

'Of course not,' said Richard and Anne, simultaneously and with vehemence. 'Where there's a will,
there's a way. That's our motto.'

Matty thanked them, and once more they climbed
the lane past the bird sanctuary and on up to the heath.
When they reached the Manor, only a few dozen books
remained to be looked into. They told the others what
they had decided, and then joined in the search.

It was Cherry who turned the pages of the very last
volume. It was half past twelve as she did so. If the will
was there, it was she who was to be allowed to find it.
But therew as nothing there – not even a bill, a letter,
or an odd scrap of paper, much less the last will and
testament of Stephen Beverly Jay.

The search had failed. There was nothing to do but
to admit it and accept defeat. Deborah was silent and
thoughtful. Anne and Cherry were almost in tears. The
boys had nothing to say.

It was time to be getting back to lunch. Even if there
had been any more books to look at, Winston and
Beaver could not come in the afternoon. They had an
important meeting of their scout troop to attend. Aunt
Frances had promised to take Richard and Cherry out

to tea. The search had ended. The children separated and wandered disconsolately round the library, as if hoping for a last minute inspiration. But none came, and at last they could wait no longer and went off in the direction of the barn to retrieve their cycles.

Richard and Deborah were the last to leave. As Richard stopped to lock the French windows, Deborah came up to him and said:

'I say, Richard, couldn't you come up once more this afternoon? We might have one more look – and anyway, someone ought to clean up headquarters and put these books and things tidy.'

Richard thought for a minute.

'All right,' he said. 'As a matter of fact, Cherry and I have an awfully boring tea-party to go to, but I could easily get out of it. I'll tell Aunt Frances I've got to come and clear up, and she can take Cherry. I'll meet you here at two-thirty.'

'I'll be ready. Will you call at the house? Shall we ask Anne? There's quite a bit to do. She may be free.'

But Anne was not free. Her father was having the day off before starting a new job in Mulcaster, and he had borrowed a motor-cycle and sidecar to take his wife and daughter to the sea for the afternoon. Mrs Shipley had once more been far from well, and Anne wanted to be with her.

So in the afternoon, for the last time, Richard and Deborah cycled up to the Manor together, let themselves into the library and silently, without enthusiasm, began to tidy up the books and papers. They had agreed to go and report failure to Matty after tea, for she had said she would be out during the afternoon. It was something they were not looking forward to.

It was a terribly hot day. The heat-wave seemed to

have reached its climax, and there was thunder in the air. To work in such heat was almost unbearable. More than once Deborah sank with a deep sigh into her favourite chair at the painted bureau, laid her head on her arms on the open lid, and nearly fell asleep. Richard worked methodically at the piles of papers and scattered volumes. At last Deborah said:

'Would it be very mean of me to go and have a nap in the garden? I just can't keep awake. I didn't sleep very well after the moonlight feast last night. I expect I'll be all right in half an hour.'

'O.K.,' said Richard. 'Go ahead. We can finish off later when it's not so hot.'

'Oh, thanks,' said Deborah.

Then she sauntered out to her favourite spot under some trees in the paddock. There she could see the old brick walls of the Manor, watch the butterflies lazily dancing overhead, and hear the peaceful sound of Dragon munching grass not many yards away. It was only a few minutes before she was asleep.

Richard, meanwhile, having made the library more or less tidy, went across to the barn to clear up the remains of their last headquarters.

How long Deborah slept she did not know, but as she slept she dreamed.

It seemed as if she was in a world at once strange and somehow familiar. The sun was shining, a number of sheep were straying in a green meadow, and ladies and gentlemen in stiff brocades and silks were posing beneath the trees, while the sheep grazed the short, neat turf and bleated as they moved. She herself, dressed in a white silk gown and carrying a shepherdess's crook, was mounted on a huge brown charger. All this seemed perfectly natural. She was looking for someone. Her horse wandered here and there in the landscape, while she peered at the faces of the gentlemen about her. They were not all so pleasant as their charming, old-world costumes would have led her to suppose. The first gentleman she looked at, examined closely, displayed, beneath a white periwig, a face not unlike that of Seedy. She gave her horse's rein a tug and moved on. The next gentleman was uncomfortably like Dusty, and the face of the third was that of the Professor. The first was sitting under a tree with yellow flowers, stroking a white lamb; the second sat in the open, playing a flute; and the third reclined under a great chestnut tree with orange and red autumnal foliage.

'But he's under the *green* tree, isn't he, Dennis?' a voice kept saying. 'He's under the green tree.'

Deborah recognized the voice of Miss Matty, but of that lady herself there was no sign.

Then the horse turned, and towards the horizon she made out a tree with brilliant green foliage. In its shade sat a young gentleman in a pink satin jacket and white breeches. He was reading a book. Beside him Deborah could just make out more books – old, leather-bound volumes, some of them open and some closed.

'Gee up, Dragon!' she said in her dream, and the horse broke into a canter, and then into a gallop. Nearer and nearer they came to the green tree, until Deborah could make out each of its many oval leaves. Just as they were approaching it, the horse tripped; there was an unearthly crash, and Deborah screamed as she fell headlong from the horse's back.

Her dream had been broken off abruptly by a peal of thunder. Richard, hearing the crash and seeing a vivid flash of lightning, ran out of the barn to see if she was all right.

Deborah, waking suddenly, was astonished to find that a few big drops of rain had fallen upon her. She jumped up and ran to meet Richard.

'Come on!' he said. 'It's started to rain. Let's get under cover.'

'Where am I?' said Deborah. 'Oh, Richard, I've found it – I *know* I've found it.'

'You're crazy! Let's get into the barn, quick!'

'No, the library! It's in the library – I *know* it is. This way!'

She grabbed his arm and tugged him in the opposite direction.

As they reached the flagged path, the downpour caught them. But another few steps brought them to the little terrace outside the french window. Richard fumbled hastily with the door-handle, and in another moment they were inside.

They shook the rain from their hair and clothes.

'Now,' said Richard, 'what on earth are you talking about? I suppose you've been dreaming.'

In a flash Deborah had recognized the landscape of her dream – the close-cropped turf, the eighteenth-century shepherds and shepherdesses, the row of trees with their formal foliage, each of a different colour. And she *knew* – knew with absolute certainty – where the will was.

Then suddenly she felt afraid of her discovery. She dared not risk being wrong. She must make Richard find it. After all, it was he who had worked the hardest. He deserved the final triumph.

Her excitement seemed to have vanished in an instant.

'It's just an idea,' she said. 'Probably no good. It came to me as I was lying in the paddock. See this desk here? Well, sit down and have a look at it.'

She had led him across to the painted bureau. He did as he was told. In front of him the lid was open, revealing a row of pigeon-holes, now empty, where Stephen must have kept his envelopes and writing-paper. Below these was a narrow panel of carved and inlaid wood, running the whole width of the bureau. The panel depicted the landscape of Deborah's dream, with its ladies and gentlemen lolling in the shade.

'Look there,' said Deborah. 'Do you see anything? Remember what the old man kept saying to Matty? "Under the green tree."'

Richard looked at the inlaid panel. Then his eye caught the farthest tree on the right – brilliant green in contrast with the yellow and red of the others.

'It's a green tree, right enough,' he said slowly – then all at once he turned to her with a flash of understanding.

'You mean,' he said, 'it's under there – somehow. Why, yes, look there!'

'Oh, try it, Richard!' said Deborah. 'Try it – that row of knobs – surely one of them works.'

Beneath the panel was a row of little bosses or knobs, carved in wood and exactly resembling another row along the top of the panel. They appeared to be purely ornamental, but as Richard fingered the one immediately below the centre of the green tree, he found that it was loose. Before he was completely aware of what he had done, a part of the woodwork had sprung out an inch or so towards him. Attached to it were four of the knobs, and one of these, when pressed, had evidently released a hidden spring.

Richard drew out a shallow drawer; as he did so, Deborah bent forward and took out a long narrow envelope. On it was written in ink, simply, 'S. B. Jay, WILL.' The envelope was not sealed. Inside it was a folded sheet of crisp, pale blue paper inscribed: 'Last Will and Testament of Stephen Beverly Jay of Mulbridge Manor, Mulbridge, in the County of Southshire.'

They looked no further. It was not their business to read the dead man's will.

'Let's go and tell Matty,' said Deborah.

'Yes. *You* tell her. It was you who found it – your idea, anyway. . . .'

'No,' said Deborah. 'We both found it. I'd rather.'

Richard made no comment, but put the will and its envelope carefully in his breast pocket. It had stopped raining; the storm had passed, and the sun had come out once more. Against the deep blue-black clouds in the distance there was the faintest of rainbows. The air was deliciously fresh and cool.

Once more Richard locked the library, and they went for their cycles.

'Stick close to me,' said Richard, as they started off. 'We don't want to be knocked off our bikes like Winston. Keep a good look-out.'

But they reached 'Rosebank' unmolested. Ivy, the maid, told them she thought Miss Jay was upstairs in her room. They met Matty on the landing.

'We've got it,' said Richard in a low voice, patting his breast pocket. 'Can we come into your room?'

Matty was too deaf to hear what Richard said, but he repeated his question, and together they went to her room. So excited were the children that they scarcely noticed the Professor coming out of his room just as they sighted Matty. He went past them on his way downstairs with a cheerful 'Good evening'.

Once inside Matty's room with the door closed, they handed over the will, and Matty, after an agonizing delay while she found her glasses, read it through to herself. It was quite short. When she had finished reading, she looked at them with tears in her eyes:

'It's his will all right,' she said quietly, 'and he has left everything to me – except for a few hundred pounds to one or two charities he was interested in. There's no mistake about its being his will. That's Stephen's signature. I know it well. And guess who witnessed it?'

She explained briefly that in order to be legal, a signature on a will has to be witnessed by two other people.

Richard and Deborah had no idea.

'Why, Mrs Mead! That's her signature, you see. "Jessie L. Mead." She came to work for us often in the old days. It was natural Stephen should ask her to witness his signature. We might have saved ourselves a certain amount of worry, if we'd asked her. I don't suppose she'd have known it was his will she was signing, but at least she could have told us she witnessed *something*.'

'We ought to be getting home,' said Richard.

'Very well, my dears – and I suppose I should be getting ready for supper. We have it very early here, you know, on account of Ivy.'

'Whatever you do, look after the will,' urged Richard.

'Of course,' said Matty. 'See, I'll hide it in my drawer, here, and first thing in the morning I'll post it off to Stephen's solicitor in London. It's too late to catch the post tonight.'

'All right,' said Richard. 'But don't forget.'

'As if I could forget a thing like that!' said Matty gaily. 'But how am I going to thank you all? I tell you what, do you think you could get all your friends together and tomorrow we'll have a grand farewell tea-party up at the Manor. I'll ask Mrs Mead to come and help. And I expect you'll all help too, won't you?'

So it was agreed. Having told Matty briefly where they had found the will, after all hope had been given up, they once more took their leave. As they got to the door, Richard suddenly thought of something.

'I say,' he said, 'did you return the Professor his killing-bottle?'

'Not yet,' said Matty. 'I think I'll put it beside his place at supper, and see what he says. I can tell him it's for destroying anything he finds in the salad! He's jolly good fun, the Professor.'

They all laughed. None of them had felt light-hearted for days.

Within two minutes the children were speeding on their way back to Mulcaster with the news.

Chapter Fourteen

THE BIRD SANCTUARY

AND there the story should have ended. What Matty meant to do was to keep the will safely in her drawer, unknown to any but the children, write a short letter to her late brother's lawyer in London, and post it together with the will first thing next morning. But it was not to be so simple as that.

After the supper had been cleared away and washed up, her friend Mrs Mosscrop reminded her that she had promised to take a hand in a game of whist. When the game was over, she was too tired to write to the lawyer, so she put off the task until the next morning.

She overslept, and when she awoke she was delighted to find that someone had been in and left her a cup of tea with the saucer thoughtfully placed over the cup to keep it hot. No doubt this was the work of Ivy, who had taken a great liking to Matty since she had come to live at 'Rosebank'.

'Now, isn't that nice of Ivy – if it *was* Ivy?' she said. 'Don't you think that's kind and thoughtful of her, Dennis?'

Dennis, who now slept under his mistress's bed, did not answer.

'Yes, a really kind and thoughtful thing to do,' Matty continued. 'But we mustn't lie here all day, must we? Heavens! I was almost forgetting. We've got a very important letter to write, haven't we, Dennis?'

Mildly surprised to hear nothing from Dennis still, Matty looked over the edge of the bed; she leaned still farther out until she could see right under it. No Dennis! But he was certainly there last night, curled up on his own private rug. Ivy must have let him out when she brought the tea. Oh, bother the girl!

In some anxiety Matty got up and dressed. Before going in to breakfast, she had a look round the house and garden for the errant dog. There was no sign of him.

'Let's hope he's just trotted over the heath to the Manor,' said Matty to herself, as she went in to breakfast.

Afterwards she went up to her room and took out the will. There it was, safe and sound in its outer envelope. She took out pen and paper, and wrote a short note to the lawyer. She had just signed and blotted it when there was an agitated knocking at the door.

Pushing the letter and the will back into the envelope and replacing them in her drawer, she cried, 'Come in!' and, almost without waiting for an answer, Mrs Mosscrop appeared in the doorway.

'Matty, dear,' she said, 'the police inspector from Mulcaster has just rung up. He says you must go to the station at once!'

'Whatever's happened?' asked Matty, fearing the worst.

'Dennis has been getting himself into trouble again, I'm afraid. It seems he caused a motor accident on the Mulcaster road half an hour ago. The inspector's furious.'

'Is he on the phone now?' asked Matty. 'Let me speak to him.'

'No, he rang off. He said he was busy and couldn't wait. He said you were to get down there yourself in person at once, or there would be a very serious charge.'

'I'll have to go, then. Do you know when the next bus is?'

'One of the guests is going right away in his car. If you hurry, he'll give you a lift. Shall I come with you?'

'Oh no, dear, thank you. I'm used to managing things on my own. I've done it all my life.'

'Well, you'd better hurry. The car's just going.'

Matty hastily put on a coat – she never wore a hat – grasped her handbag and followed Mrs Mosscrop out of the room. Then she hesitated, took her door-key out of her bag, and locked her room. The precious will would be safe till she got back.

She hurried down the two flights of stairs, almost fell over the Professor, and was in the car in no time. The obliging guest was waiting at the front door. With Matty beside him breathlessly gasping out her gratitude, he drove off towards Mulcaster.

At the police station she was made to wait. She sat in the outer office half fuming and half anxious, until at last the inspector was free to see her.

Her arrival had been greeted by barking from some inner room, so that at least she knew that Dennis was safe. First, she had to identify him as her dog, though this was scarcely necessary.

'He's your dog all right, Miss Jay,' said the inspector. 'He's becoming not only a nuisance to us in the force, but also a danger to the public.'

'Oh dear,' said Matty. 'Please tell me about the accident. I *do* so hope no one was hurt.'

'By a miracle, no,' said the inspector. 'It seems this dog of yours ran across the road just as a car was coming. The driver swerved to avoid him, and in doing so hit a cyclist who was approaching from the opposite direction. The cycle was in a nasty mess, the car got a bent wing, and the cyclist was a bit bruised – but no bones broken. You may thank your stars for that!'

'Oh, I'm so glad,' said Matty.

'But I'm afraid that's not the last you'll hear of it. The cyclist and the driver of the car may both claim damages against you, as the owner of the dog; and I shouldn't wonder if the police ask for an order to have the dog destroyed.'

'I hope not,' said Matty earnestly. 'From now on, I'll keep him on a lead. I'll –'

'You've been warned about him before, you know,' said the inspector sternly. 'I don't suppose the magistrate will overlook it this time. Have you anything to say in your defence?'

'Dennis has always been such a good, quiet dog,' said Matty. 'It's the move that's unsettled him, you know. And then I've been so worried – I haven't been able to give him all the care he needs.'

'Oh, you've been worried,' said the inspector more kindly. 'About anything in particular, may I ask?'

Matty hesitated. She had no intention of telling the police the whole story of the will, not until it was safely in the lawyer's hands at any rate. But she might tell part of the story. Then she had an inspiration. She remembered Richard's extraordinary account of the night intruder at the Manor. She decided to tell it to the inspector: that would give the police something to think about and perhaps distract their attention a little from the misdeeds of Dennis.

'I've been worried about burglars,' she began, 'since I left the Manor – that's my house on the heath. You know it of course.'

'Oh,' said the inspector gravely, 'have you any reason to suspect burglars?'

Then Matty told him how she had given some children she knew permission to have a moonlight feast in her barn, as a reward for helping her with some sorting and tidying; how they had observed the Professor in the paddock; and how at their approach he had made a sudden disappearance. Next day, she said, the library had been found in disorder, though nothing was actually missing. She had not intended, when she began her story, to give the Professor away; but, as Richard had said, she scarcely knew him, and indeed he might be someone the police ought to know about. And after all, although the will was now safe, there *had* been nocturnal trespassers at the Manor, and undoubtedly they had been up to no good.

The inspector found Matty's story a strange one, and he made it obvious that he was not too ready to believe everything she said. He asked her a great many questions and made some notes in a note-book, and then he said she might go, but he would undoubtedly be calling to see her again.

'You'd better say nothing to this Doctor – what's his name? – Eastwell – the man you call "the Professor",' the inspector warned her. 'I'll have a word with him. Perhaps he can tell us some more. You can take the dog with you *this* time, but mind – you must keep a sharp eye on him. Tie him up if necessary. Take my advice, and don't let him off the lead. Good day for the present.'

Matty said good day to the inspector and walked out, holding Dennis by the piece of rope which the police had obligingly fixed to his collar.

She went to the nearest pet store and bought him a new lead. He had one somewhere, but Matty seemed to have mislaid it in the move, and she really could not take him about on a piece of string! Then she felt tired, and went into the Corner Café for a cup of coffee and some biscuits. She had to wait a while for a bus back to Mulbridge, and when she reached 'Rosebank', it was already time for lunch.

When lunch was over, Matty climbed once more to her room. The day was by now so hot that she felt overcome. It had been a tiring and vexatious morning. She really could not go out again until she had had a rest. Taking off her shoes she lay down on the bed. It was nearly three o'clock when her nap ended. She made sure that Dennis was still with her, and was relieved to find him snoozing penitently in his place under the bed. She must post the letter to the lawyer, and then – goodness, yes! she had almost forgotten about the tea-party to which she had invited the children to celebrate the triumphant conclusion of their long search.

She took the envelope from her drawer, glanced once more at the will, and at the letter she had written, and sealed the envelope. Then she addressed and stamped it.

Suddenly she remembered it was early closing day in the village. The Post Office-cum-Newspaper-Shop-cum-Tobacconist-cum-General Store would be shut. She could not register the letter unless she took it into Mulcaster. The thought of another journey to the city that afternoon appalled her. Fortunately, Matty had never been a strong believer in the registered post. She had always said that it was as good a way of getting anything stolen as any other; she had never lost anything she had put in the ordinary post, and there was no reason why this letter should be lost just because it contained a will. Besides, if she went into Mulcaster, she could not possibly get the children's tea ready in time; as it was, she would have to borrow some orange squash and some cakes from her hostess, Mrs Mosscrop. As for the letter, she would drop it into the box she used nearly every time she wrote a letter – the one in the lane leading up to the heath. There was, she knew, a collection at about three-forty-five. She could catch this easily, and make sure that the letter reached London the following morning. Then she would go on up to the Manor, where Mrs Mead had promised to help with the tea-party.

So, not long after three o'clock Matty set off with a big bag full of cakes and orange squash in one hand, and in the other her handbag containing the letter, and one end of Dennis's new lead. At last her adventures seemed to be nearing their conclusion.

Meanwhile, another event had been taking place – something entirely unconnected with wills, manor houses, and inquisitive strangers.

Two very respectable young men, from a most respectable institution – no less than the British Broadcasting Corporation – had that morning arrived at Mulbridge in a smart van containing some most complicated and up-to-date apparatus. The young men called one another 'Humphrey' and 'Fred'. Humphrey was an expert on bird-song; Fred was the recording engineer.

The B.B.C. was at that time broadcasting a series of recorded programmes giving actual examples of British birds, month by month. The month of August, as any naturalist will admit, is a lean time for collecting the songs of birds. Most of the more tuneful have begun to take a holiday before either migrating or else tuning up for the autumn season. But Mulbridge Woods are famous as a bird sanctuary. Elsewhere the blackcap and the blackbird have become almost silent by the end of July: at Mulbridge they still sing on. The trill of the hedge-sparrow, and its occasional plaintive piping, can be heard to perfection; at Mulbridge too you may hear the laugh of the green woodpecker on the wing, and the lively twittering of the goldfinch; while the rippling tinkle of the blue tit, in some places not heard until late August, begins earlier there than anywhere else in the south of England.

In short, Humphrey had agreed with his bird-loving colleagues that if any good recordings were to be made in August, it would assuredly be in Mulbridge Woods.

That morning the two young men had driven the van at a leisurely pace up the deserted lane that skirts the wood, and had noticed a particularly charming patch of sunlight at a point where the scarlet of one of Her Majesty's letter-boxes made a vivid splash against the background of dark green. Beside it was a rustic seat consisting of a single ancient, weathered plank nailed across two supports which were driven into the ground. Opposite, across the lane, were some scrubby gorse bushes bordering the lower slopes of the heath. Humphrey got out of the van and sat on the rustic seat, while Fred remained at the wheel, ready to do as his companion ordered. Nothing disturbed the warm, morning air but the gentle cooing of a wood-pigeon high in the trees that overhung the lane, and the various songs of three or four other birds in the hedge or on near-by branches.

'Couldn't be better,' said Humphrey, whose expert ear had already identified two or three. 'We'll place the Number One mike here, old boy.'

'Good show,' said Fred. 'What about Number Two?'

'Could we drive on a bit up the lane?' suggested Humphrey.

A hundred yards or so farther on they stopped once more. Both got out this time, and climbing through a gap in the hedge, made their way some distance into the wood itself.

Again Humphrey listened.

'What about placing Number Two here?' he said.

'Jolly good,' said Fred, noting the distance from the place selected for Number One. They had plenty of cable.

'Now for Number Three,' said Humphrey.

Once more a suitable spot was chosen; the next problem was to decide where to park the recording van. Fortunately a convenient site was found just off the lane, where there had once been a gateway, long since closed up when the wood had been made a sanctuary. It had the advantage of being well hidden from the lane in case of intruders, and from the places decided upon for the three microphones. These were the most sensitive obtainable, and although they had the disadvantage of picking up a good deal of background noise, they would also record faithfully any song-bird that performed within a radius of many yards. Having three microphones, all connected to the same recording apparatus, the engineer would be able instantly to switch from one to another in case the birds within range of one of them should go silent.

The positions decided, it remained to place the three microphones and wire them to the van. This took much patient labour; first, the two microphones in the wood itself were connected, and then the young men tackled the one in the hedge near the pillar-box. Not only was it necessary to conceal the apparatus from the birds, who could so easily become suspicious; it had also to be hidden from chance passers-by, who might interfere with it while the two young men were inside the van.

At last, however, everything was satisfactorily installed.

'Shall we test now, old boy,' asked Fred, 'or eat first?'

'Don't mind,' said Humphrey. 'What do you say?'

'What about going down to the village for a spot of lunch and coming back to do our stuff later?'

'Suits me. Do you suppose one can get a bite in the village?'

'I noticed a place called "Rosebank" or something. Didn't look *too* unlikely. It had a board up saying meals were served to non-residents. It's not far down the lane.'

'Sounds pretty dubious,' said Humphrey. 'Couldn't unhitch the van, I suppose, and go back to Mulcaster?'

'Not a chance,' replied Fred, 'because (*a*) we can't leave the mikes lying around all that time, and (*b*) it's late already, and if I know anything about the hostelries of Mulcaster, they won't serve anything worth eating by the time we get there.'

'All right, old boy, better chance ye local guestehouse. I can walk it, if you can – just about; it's a scorcher and no error.'

'Good show. Let's beat it, then. I don't much like leaving the stuff, but I guess it's safe enough. Doubt if six people use this lane from year's end to year's end.'

They strolled down the lane, and before long the obliging Ivy was setting before them, late though it was for lunch, some excellent clear soup, cold meat, salad and new potatoes, followed by ice-cream and coffee. Well contented, the young men lingered over their cigarettes. At length they got up, thanked the waitress for their meal, paid the bill, and returned to the recording-van. Everything was as they had left it.

Humphrey went from microphone to microphone, speaking quietly and calmly into each in turn, while Fred, inside the van, adjusted the controls.

'Hullo, Fred,' Humphrey would say, 'hullo, hullo. One, two, three, four, five, six, seven, eight, nine, ten. I am now six feet from the mike,' and so on.

When all three microphones had been tested, he rejoined his companion in the van; and by the time Matty had left the guest-house in the company of Dennis, the two young men were seated in the van listening through headphones to the delightful trilling and twittering of the Mulbridge singers. It took some time to tune in each microphone to Humphrey's satisfaction. He was an artist, and his bird-song programmes were justly famous. He was not going to spoil the August one for the sake of saving ten minutes or so. In due time, however, when reception was as nearly perfect as it could be, and a sufficient number of birds were busy at their matinée performance, Humphrey gave Fred the signal to begin recording.

Chapter Fifteen

HER MAJESTY'S MAIL

THE events of the previous day had not gone un-
noticed by Mr Gerald Jay's hired malefactors, Seedy
and Dusty. They had guessed that the search by the
children was nearing its end. From a safe distance they
had watched Richard and Deborah visit Miss Jay at
'Rosebank' the evening before. It was not the children's usual time for paying calls. Had they in fact
brought the missing document? That, of course, they
could not know. If it were so, their chance of getting
it was slender. Nevertheless, until the will was actually
in the possession of Matty's London lawyer, there was
still a hope of stealing and destroying it.

Next morning they were up early. Since things had
evidently reached a critical stage, they determined to
expend some of their hard-earned wages in hiring a
car, which would certainly be useful, if not indispen-
sable. In any case, both of them had had enough of
tramping about the countryside on foot in the boiling
August sun. They drove to Mulbridge and parked the
hired car at a convenient distance from 'Rosebank',
and then concealed themselves to watch events.

The first thing of importance they noticed was the
departure of Matty in the direction of Mulcaster in a
car belonging to one of the guests at 'Rosebank'. As
soon as this car was well on its way, they followed.
They were surprised when Matty was dropped at the
entrance to the police station. Matty's driver then
turned his car and drove off, while Matty herself

entered the forbidding doors. Through those doors the
gentlemen now concealed in the hired car had no intention of following her. They preferred to wait until she
emerged.

When a quarter of an hour had passed and still she
did not appear, they decided that one of them should
wait and keep a look-out, while the other paid a rapid
visit to the Manor by car to see what was happening
there. They could not imagine why Matty was calling on
the police. She could scarcely be handing them the will.
The most natural thing for her to be doing, if the will
was in her possession, was either to catch a train for
London, or, as was more likely, to pay a visit to the
General Post Office, where she could send it to London
by registered post.

Still puzzling over this, Seedy drove off towards the
Manor, while Dusty lurked in the narrow lanes about
the police station. He was still awaiting Matty's appearance when Seedy returned.

'Has the old lady come out yet?' asked Seedy.

'No,' answered Dusty, 'not a sign of her. Whatever she's doing in there, it's taking her a darned long
time.'

'Well, there's nothing to do but wait.'

'Did you get to the Manor?'

'Yeah.'

'Anything interesting?'

'Yeah – think so. Tell you what – I think those kids
have knocked off – given the game up. There wasn't a
soul there, so I had a snoop round. Their headquarters
– you know, that barn we went over – has been packed
up. All their stuff's gone!'

'You don't say.'

'And I had a look into the library. It's all been tidied

up, and it looks as though they'd finished in there. Can't understand it.'

'Well,' said Dusty, 'it looks as if they'd turned it in. Either they've given up trying, or they've found it.'

'There's only one thing to do,' Seedy said. 'Keep our eyes on the old dame. Hullo! there she is.'

Matty did indeed, at that moment, emerge from the doors of the police station. She had her old black retriever on a piece of rope. It was fortunate that they had not noticed whether she had been with Dennis on entering the station, or they might have guessed at the reason for her visit. Their view of her had not been good at the moment when she had got out of the car belonging to the guest from 'Rosebank'.

From a safe distance they surveyed the rest of her movements during the remaining half hour or so in Mulcaster. They saw her go into the pet shop and come out with a new dog lead. They saw her go into the Corner Café, and Dusty slipped inside to see what she was up to. Buying a packet of cigarettes at the cash desk, he observed that she was up to nothing more unusual than sipping a cup of coffee, with Dennis reclining beside her chair.

She was certainly *not* going to the General Post Office. Instead, they saw her join the small queue outside the Town Hall which was waiting for the Mulbridge bus.

Then Seedy had an idea.

'Come on,' he said. 'No use waiting here. She's going to get the bus in five minutes. That means she'll be home in half an hour or less. We've just time to have a look at her room – if we're lucky.'

Before Dusty could properly grasp this daring plan, Seedy had already pressed the starter button, put the engine in gear, and trodden on the accelerator. He drove very fast into Mulbridge, and they parked the car not far from 'Rosebank' and approached the guesthouse on foot.

Just how they were to get into Matty's room on the second floor Seedy had not decided. It might prove altogether too risky; on the other hand, the risk might be worth taking.

They entered the lounge and asked Ivy for two cups of coffee.

'It's a bit near lunch time,' she said. 'We don't usually serve coffee after twelve. But if you wait a minute, I'll see what I can do.'

While she was gone, Seedy stepped casually into the hall to see if anyone was about. The house appeared to be deserted. He knew whereabouts Matty's room was, from having overheard her talking to Mrs Mosscrop on his previous visit to the guest-house. He hesitated for an instant, then darted upstairs.

Ivy returned to the lounge.

'I'm sorry,' she said. 'There's no coffee made, and we shan't be making any more until after lunch. Will you be wanting a meal?'

'I'll ask my friend,' said Dusty. 'He just stepped outside for a minute.'

'No thanks, miss,' said Seedy, who had at that moment reappeared at the door of the lounge. 'We can't stop to lunch.'

Ivy said she was sorry, and the two men went out.

'Find out anythink?' asked Dusty.

'No,' said Seedy, 'only that she keeps her door locked.'

'Hullo!' said Dusty suddenly, touching his companion on the arm. 'Who's this?'

They were walking up the lane towards the hired car, but the appearance of a newcomer approaching the guest-house made them pause and turn their heads.

It was the Professor.

'Don't like that bird,' said Dusty. 'Pops up all over the place, he does. Shouldn't wonder if he's up to no good.'

'Let's beat it,' said Seedy.

They continued rapidly up the lane, and a quick glance round showed them the Professor disappearing through the gateway of 'Rosebank'.

When they hired the car in Mulcaster, they had taken the precaution of bringing food with them. They drove along a bumpy track leading on to the heath, and in a sheltered spot, from which, with a pair of field-glasses, they could observe the front of the guest-house, they sat down and had lunch. Very soon they made out the figure of Matty, with Dennis on his lead, entering the doorway of 'Rosebank'. She had evidently just walked up from the bus stop in the village.

'She'll have lunch now,' said Seedy, 'and after that a nap, I dare say.'

'I wouldn't mind taking a nap myself,' said Dusty. 'It's a fair scorcher.'

He mopped his forehead with a soiled handkerchief and let himself roll gently over on to the cool shady grass.

'Do as you like,' said Seedy, 'only don't snore.'

Seedy kept an eye on 'Rosebank'. Without in the least knowing who they were, he noticed, among other casual arrivals for lunch, the two gentlemen from the B.B.C. He also saw them reappear an hour later, and make off up the lane.

'Look there,' he said. 'I don't like that.'

He handed Dusty the field-glasses. Through them he had seen a dark shiny car drive up to 'Rosebank' and stop at the gate. It did not take him long to recognize a police car. A man in dark blue uniform got out of the car and went up the steps to the house.

'Here, give me back the glasses,' said Seedy, when Dusty had had a good look.

'What are the police doing there?' asked Dusty.

'Search me. I guess we'd better make ourselves scarce. Bad enough having kids messing around, but when the police join in, it's no place for you and I.'

Then, through the glasses, he saw the police officer come out of the house, accompanied by none other than the Professor. The Professor seemed to be arguing with him, but the officer refused to listen. Both got into the police car, which turned rapidly and disappeared in the direction of Mulcaster. Peace returned to 'Rosebank'.

'Tell you what,' said Seedy, half an hour later. 'Not much good sticking here. I've got an idea. Suppose the old dame's got the will and hasn't sent it off yet. Either she'll have to go back to Mulcaster, which isn't very likely, seeing she's already been once today; or she'll have to shove it into the ordinary letter-box, on account of the post office being shut today in the village.'

'So what?'

'So we might keep an eye on the pillar-box up the lane. I've watched that old girl, and several times I've seen her leave the house after her forty winks and trot up the road with a couple of letters for the post. After that, she generally goes on to the Manor. She always sticks her letters in the box up the lane.'

'There's just a chance,' agreed Dusty. 'What do we

do? Hide in the hedge and knock her on the head when she turns up?'

'Shan't have to knock her on the head. I don't suppose she'll give much trouble.'

'What time does the post go?'

'About a quarter to four. It's after three now. She generally leaves the house about now. Let's go.'

There was a spot on the heath a little higher up where they were only a few yards from the road opposite the pillar-box, and from where, with the field-glasses, they could still just make out the front of the guest-house. They could not take the car, for the ground was too uneven, but the spot was only a few minutes' distance away on foot. Before leaving the car, however, a sudden idea occurred to Seedy. He opened one of the doors of the car and stooped to bring out something that lay inside, on the back seat. It was a small leather case. He opened the case, drew out something which he stowed in his side pocket, and threw the case back on the seat of the car. Closing the door carefully, he joined Dusty, and together they made for the place opposite the pillar-box.

They settled themselves as comfortably as they could behind the scrubby bushes bordering the lane. Opposite was the pillar-box with the rough wayside seat beside it. Away to their left, they could just make out 'Rosebank' and part of the lane above it.

Soon after this Matty came down the steps of the guest-house with Dennis on a lead in front of her. Her handbag was in one hand, and her bag full of provisions in the other. Slowly she proceeded up the lane.

She had not gone far before someone hailed her. Matty stopped in her walk and turned to look down the road. It was the comfortable figure of Mrs Mead.

'Miss Jay! Oh, Miss Jay!' she called out, panting hard as she ran. 'Wait for me – I'll – come with – you.'

Matty waited. As soon as Mrs Mead was well within earshot, she said:

'Of course – you're coming up to the Manor to help with the tea-party, aren't you? I'll be delighted to walk along with you. Take it easy. There's no great hurry.'

Mrs Mead puffed up to Matty, and the other allowed her time to get her breath before starting off once more.

'Doesn't do me no good, running at my time of life,' said Mrs Mead. 'Here, give me the bag.'

Matty gladly yielded to her the bag of provisions.

A few minutes later they reached the wayside pillar-box. 'Just a minute,' said Matty. 'I mustn't forget to post my letter.'

All, or most, of this was watched with consternation by the two in the bushes. Matty alone would have been no problem; Matty and her dog together they might have managed; but Matty and the dog and Mrs Mead, who looked no weakling, were more than Seedy and Dusty cared to risk. It was no good. Powerless to interfere, they watched the little party stop at the pillar-box across the lane; then they saw Matty open her hand-bag, take out a long envelope, stamped and sealed, and drop it safely into the box. They heard Matty say:

'There! That's that, and I'm glad to get it off my hands. Now I can think about having those dear children to tea.'

As soon as the two ladies and the dog were out of sight, Seedy turned to his companion with a look of baffled determination on his face.

'Well, there's only one thing for it now. In about quarter of an hour, the postman'll turn up. He comes on his cycle. I've seen him. If we can't get the letter from the old girl, we'll have to get it from the postman.'

'Risky,' said Dusty. 'Serious offence if they catch us.'

'Pray God nobody comes along and messes things up this time,' said Seedy.

They emerged from the bushes and crossed the lane, looking casually to right and to left as they did so. There was no one in sight. If they were going to rob the postman, they had better be as near the pillar-box as possible. The more boldly they acted, the less they would be suspect.

They sat down on the rough seat beside the pillar-box. Dusty took a frayed newspaper from his pocket and handed the inside sheet to his companion. For a minute, both read in silence.

'What's the time?' asked Dusty.

'Ten minutes to go, I make it,' said Seedy. 'He's not usually late.'

'What are we going to do?'

'I'm not taking any chances,' said Seedy. 'I've got the stuff in my pocket.'

He patted the side of his jacket.

'He's an oldish chap,' he went on, 'and we'd better not use violence. Don't want to risk a murder charge.'

There was another brief silence.

'Wish he'd get a move on,' said Dusty. 'I don't like this hanging about. Anybody may come along. Next time, Mr Gerald Jay can do his own dirty business. Why isn't he here to help us?'

'It doesn't suit him. He might be recognized. He's paid us to do it for him, hasn't he?'

'When we get the will,' said Dusty, 'that is, *if* we get the will, what are we going to do with it?'

'If it's like this and there's nobody about, we'll hop into the car and take it to Gerald. If there's anybody about, we'll get rid of it. He said he'd pay us just the same.'

'There'll be a big stink, you know. The police'll be after us. Hadn't we better take the postman with us and keep him quiet till we're out of the way?'

'Don't like kidnapping,' said Seedy. 'We'll take a chance. By this time tomorrow we'll be in Holland. Gerald's fixed it.'

'The whole thing's too darned shaky for my liking. I wish –'

'Shut your mouth!' said Seedy all of a sudden. 'Here he comes!'

From the next bend along the lane came the ting-a-ling of a cycle bell. The two men buried their faces in their newspapers, and out of the corner of his eye each of them caught sight of the stout form of the village postman approaching on a faded red bicycle.

Ted Hoskins, perspiring freely, applied his brakes and dismounted a yard or two from the pillar-box. He was accustomed to lean his cycle against the plank seat while he cleared the box, but as it was occupied at this moment by a couple of strangers, he was obliged to lay his cycle on the ground at the roadside.

'Good day,' he said. 'Warm afternoon.'

The strangers said nothing, and Mr Hoskins, who was not going to force his conversation on anyone who was not disposed to be friendly, took out his keys, and bent down to unlock the box.

Instantly Seedy stepped up behind him, removing a large, crumpled handkerchief from his side pocket. Simultaneously Dusty grasped the postman's elbows from behind, and Seedy pressed the handkerchief to his nose.

'Hey!' cried Hoskins. 'What are you –'

But nothing further of his muffled cry of alarm was heard. Seedy had considerable strength, and so had the chloroform with which the handkerchief was soaked. Presently the postman's form became limp. Seedy and Dusty lifted him a few yards up the lane and laid him in a dry ditch, well overgrown with bracken.

'What about this?' said Dusty, indicating the postman's bicycle.

'Leave it,' ordered Seedy, opening the pillar-box and removing the contents. 'It won't take two minutes to go through this lot.'

They sat down on the plank seat and Seedy read the addresses on the three letters which, together with a picture postcard, were all that the box had contained.

'Here we are,' he said, looking at the long envelope. He tore it open.

' "S.B.J. Will,"' he read. Then he looked at the will itself. ' "Last will and testament,"' he continued, ' "of Stephen Beverly Jay of Mulbridge Manor, Mulbridge, in the County of Southshire." Let's see. Yes, this is what we want. "Clause 3. I give, devise, and bequeath all my real and the residue of my personal estate and effects to my said sister absolutely."'

'That's all we want to know,' said Dusty impatiently. 'We'd better not hang around.'

Seedy pushed the document into his breast pocket.

'Come on,' he said. 'Let's beat it. Here, shove these back in the box.'

They ran across the lane and on to the heath. The hired car was only a few hundred yards off.

All at once the two men caught sight of three figures coming across the heath towards them.

'I'm going to get rid of this,' said Seedy, taking the will from his pocket. 'I know them. They'll find that postman and get the police on to us in no time. Can't risk being found with this! Give me your matches, quick!'

They bent down near the ground, Seedy pushed the crumpled paper and its envelope into a tuft of dead grass, and Dusty set fire to it. In a few seconds the dry grass was blazing, and the paper had caught fire. The two men waited just long enough to see the last corner of it burn black, and then they both began running in the direction of their car.

Chapter Sixteen

FIRE ON THE HEATH

RICHARD had spent part of the morning visiting first Anne, then Beaver, to tell them the story of the discovery of the will, of how it had been handed over to Matty the evening before, and of her promise to post it to London first thing in the morning. Deborah had of course undertaken to tell her brother. Everyone was amazed and overjoyed. Richard and Deborah had agreed, before they parted, to swear them all to continued secrecy until Matty should lift the ban. There seemed to be no reason now why all Mulcaster and Mulbridge should not know of the children's triumph, since it would mean so much to the neighbourhood and to the whole county. Nevertheless, it was Matty's business to tell the news. Meanwhile, they had all been summoned to tea at the Manor.

Richard and Cherry decided to set off early after lunch, in order to go by way of Mulbridge and pick up Anne. They reached the Shipleys' cottage only to find that Anne had that morning punctured her front tyre in a frantic dash to the shops just before lunch. It was early closing day, and Mrs Shipley had run out of both flour and sugar.

'Never mind,' said Richard. 'Don't let's stop and mend it now. We can all walk together. We'll take the short cut over the heath.'

So it happened that, about the time when Seedy and Dusty were waiting for the arrival of the village postman, the three children set off from the Shipleys' cottage to cross the lower corner of the heath by a footpath which joined the lane just above the roadside pillar-box.

They were a little surprised to notice a dark blue saloon car parked on a track leading from the lane to the heath. They supposed it belonged to some holiday picnicking party, though the heath was not often used for this purpose on weekdays.

Then, beyond the car, on the horizon, Richard saw two familiar figures. What on earth could their old friends, Seedy and Dusty, be doing scrambling through the bushes on to the heath at this time?

The men appeared to have caught sight of the children. They both stopped, and Seedy took out of his pocket something white – it might be a long white envelope. He stooped down, and a moment later Richard could just make out a tongue of flame leaping from the white thing, which Seedy had half buried in the grass. The men were burning something! A tall flame, pale in the sunlight and topped with a wisp of smoke, was quite plain to see.

What on earth could they be burning – here, and in such a hurry? Then all of a sudden the truth struck Richard with terrible swiftness. They had somehow got hold of the will – perhaps they had robbed Matty's room – and on catching sight of the children, had decided to destroy it on the spot.

'Come on, Anne!' Richard cried. 'We've got to stop them. Cherry, you stay here. Hi! stop! What are you doing?'

With Anne beside him, he raced across the rising ground towards the two men. But it was too late. Before the children were within fifty yards the envelope containing the will was burnt to ashes. The grass around it was on fire. Seedy and Dusty had begun running down the slope towards the children, behind whom was parked the hired car.

'Get out of the way, you kids,' roared Seedy, 'or you'll be hurt!'

'You're too late!' growled Dusty, as he rushed past Richard, almost knocking him to the ground.

'Oh, look out, Richard!' shouted Anne.

The two men were running like mad across the grass and had almost reached their car when Richard turned to follow them. They got in, Seedy took the wheel, pressed the starter button and crashed the engine into gear. In a few seconds the car was careering down the track towards the lane. The door on Dusty's side flew open, and he put out his arm and drew it shut with a violent slam. Richard and Anne rushed to the edge of the heath in time to see the dark blue saloon swerve suddenly to the right and disappear up the side-turning that skirted Mulbridge Woods.

That was the last they saw of it.

'CPP 639,' said Richard. 'Don't forget that. We've got their number anyway. That's something. What shall we do next?'

'Better go and tell Matty,' said Anne. 'We must find out if she posted the will.'

'Better get on to the police first,' said Richard. 'Come on – there's a phone at "Rosebank".'

Cherry had joined them, and together the children ran down the lane to the guest-house.

'Please,' said Richard to the maid, who came to the door in answer to his agitated knocking, 'can I use the telephone? I want to ring the police. It's frightfully urgent.'

Ivy led him to the telephone.

'Here you are,' she said. 'Help yourself. Mrs Moss-crop's out, but I expect it'll be all right.'

While he was waiting to get through, it occurred to him to wonder what he was going to say to the police.

'Hullo, hullo!' he said. An inspiration had come just in time. 'Is that the police? I've just seen two men set fire to the heath opposite Mulbridge Woods. They got away in a dark blue saloon car, number CPP 639. They took the lane by the side of the woods in the direction of South Bentley. You'd better get after them right away! . . . What? Yes, I'm ringing from Mulbridge – "Rosebank" Guest-House . . . That's right.'

He rang off.

'They're going to send out and try to stop the car,' he said. 'They'll be coming up here soon. We'd better get to the Manor now and find the others.'

Further surprises awaited them.

Not only had a considerable fire been started among the dry undergrowth and dead ferns and bushes on the heath, but two young men were standing over something beside the pillar-box in the lane.

'What's up?' asked Richard.

'Any of you know anything about this?' asked one of the young men.

He indicated the dazed and almost unconscious form of Postman Hoskins, whom he and his companion had succeeded in removing from the ditch and getting to the seat beside the pillar-box.

'They won't know anything about it, Fred,' said the other. 'Where can we get some water? Something very funny going on here.'

'Where's the nearest house?' asked Fred.

' "Rosebank," ' answered Richard. 'It's about quarter of a mile down the lane.'

'That's the place where we had lunch, Humphrey,' said Fred. 'Better run this poor chap down there in the van.'

'O.K., old boy. You go and turn the van, and I'll stay and see to him. Can you disconnect all right?'

'Sure. Back in two shakes.'

Fred ran off up the lane to where the recording van was parked.

By this time two or three people, attracted by the huge columns of black smoke rising from the fire on the heath, had arrived on the scene. With the aid of sticks they were trying to beat out the flames, but, almost without rain for several weeks, the heath was blazing furiously.

Fred returned with the small, neat B.B.C. van.

'Better see if we can get him on to the seat beside me,' he said. 'Too much stuff in the back. Can you walk down?'

'Sure. Don't want to mess up anything in the back. We've got some very interesting bird recordings in there.'

'I'll say,' agreed Fred, helping to lift the still limp figure of Ted Hoskins into the seat beside the steering-wheel.

Very soon the three men and the three children were in the lounge at 'Rosebank'. A small but interested crowd had joined them, and on the way down they had passed other men and women on their way to try to put out the fire.

The postman, who was breathing with difficulty, was given brandy-and-water to moisten his parched lips and restore his strength. Presently he recovered sufficiently to speak.

'What happened?' he asked.

'That's what we want to know, old chap,' answered Humphrey kindly. 'You're all right. You've been doped, I think. How do you feel?'

'A bit sick,' answered the postman, 'and sort of dazed like. Where am I?'

It was Richard who explained.

'I'm beginning to remember,' said Hoskins. 'I'd just unlocked the box when these two chaps on the seat came round behind me. I tried to get away, but they were too much for me. One of them stuffed a handkerchief with some strong-smelling stuff on it into my face, and that's all I know. What were they up to?'

'Robbing the mail,' said Humphrey. 'Not your fault, old chap. Blamed rotten luck, if you ask me. Hullo, who's this?'

A black car had driven rapidly up to the house. Out of it stepped a police sergeant, accompanied by the Professor.

The police sergeant took charge. He questioned the postman and the B.B.C. men, while the Professor talked to Richard and Anne.

'So you saw them burn the will?' he asked.

'Oh, you know all about it,' said Richard.

'A good deal. I'll tell you soon. I think I can explain –'

He was cut short by the strident clanging of a bell coming rapidly nearer. A fire-engine passed the house at high speed. The interested onlookers transferred their attention to the latest excitement, running out of the house to follow the engine up the lane.

When the noise had subsided, the sergeant took a statement from Richard. He related everything that had happened from the moment he had first caught sight of Seedy and Dusty on the heath.

'Well,' concluded the sergeant, 'there's nothing more I can do at present. Mr Hoskins has told me all he can. He's all right now, and I can run him home on my way back to the station. We'll keep in touch with you, sir, if you'll tell me where you're going to be.'

'Thank you, sergeant,' said the Professor. 'I rather think I shall be up at the Manor for the next half hour or so.'

The sergeant helped the still dazed postman to the police car and took his leave. The Professor turned to the B.B.C. men.

'I wonder,' he said, 'if you gentlemen could possibly find time to drive us up to the Manor. It's only a mile or so up the lane. We can sit on each other's laps. I really think we ought to find Miss Jay and tell her what's happened.'

'What about it, Fred?' asked Humphrey, rather doubtfully.

'We can try,' said Fred. 'Seems the only way of finding out what in the name of Dick Turpin is going on around here. We can make room somehow. Tell you what, though – we can't leave the mikes and all that cable decorating the landscape. There may be other strange characters lurking around for all we know.'

'Suppose I stay behind while you run these folk up to the moated grange, old boy,' suggested Humphrey.

'No, look here – *you* drive. I'll stay behind and start dismantling the stuff. I'm better at these rough mechanic's jobs than you are.'

So it was agreed. The Professor and the children were packed into the recording van. Fred set off up the lane to see to the microphones and cable, and Humphrey turned the recording van and drove to the

Manor. On their way, they noticed that the fire brigade, together with a party of local volunteers, were at least preventing the fire from spreading.

At the Manor the others were wondering what had become of Richard, Cherry, and Anne. Matty and Mrs Mead had arrived to find Deborah and Winston waiting for them, and they were soon joined by Beaver. The five of them had prepared as good a tea as they could contrive. Dennis was padding round, sharing the general excitement and getting in everyone's way. Deborah decked her beloved Dragon with a bunch of assorted ribbons in honour of the occasion.

Matty told the children how she had, that very afternoon, posted the will to London.

'The postman must have collected it by now,' she said, 'and very soon it'll be on its way. What a wonderful day this has been – a truly wonderful day, hasn't it, Dennis? Should I ring up the County Medical Officer and tell him, I wonder? Now where can the others be? It's getting on for five.'

'They've probably had a puncture,' said Winston.

'Or two punctures,' supplemented Beaver. 'Very brainy chap, Richard, but when it comes to mending punctures, he's on the slow side.'

Speculation was beginning to give way to hunger. When Matty suggested they should make a start without the others, the boys were visibly interested. So Matty and the three children sat down at the long refectory table in the panelled dining-room, while Mrs Mead poured out orange squash. Matty had just told the children to help themselves when the door-bell jangled and Dennis responded with a bark.

Richard, without waiting for an answer, burst into the house, followed by Anne and Cherry.

'There's two men at the door,' he told Matty. 'Can they come to tea as well? Will there be enough?'

'I expect so,' said Matty. 'There are plenty of buns anyway, and I can soon make another pot of tea.'

The Professor and Humphrey joined the party in the dining-room.

'You'll be surprised to see *me* here, Miss Jay,' said the Professor. 'But I can explain everything.'

'Nothing surprises me,' answered Matty. 'Oh yes, to be sure, didn't I report you to the police this morning for breaking into my house? Why aren't you in prison?'

The general uproar, however, made conversation impossible. Humphrey, the B.B.C. man, introduced himself, and Richard, Anne, and Cherry all greeted their friends with voluble and incoherent accounts of the momentous events which had just taken place.

When at last it became understood that Richard had actually seen Stephen Jay's will burnt on Mulbridge Heath, there was a general silence – the silence of utter consternation. He could not be perfectly certain that it *was* the will, but at any rate, if Matty had just posted it in that very pillar-box, and if Seedy and Dusty had really robbed the mail, then it looked very much as if the paper with which they had set fire to the heath *must* have been the will.

'I think this is where I can help,' said Humphrey, 'if a stranger may be allowed to butt in. By an amazing coincidence, my colleague and I had placed a microphone right behind that pillar-box for the purpose of recording the Mulbridge birds for the radio. We got a most interesting recording, which I shall have the pleasure of playing to you when my engineer friend turns up. I daren't touch the apparatus without Fred –

it would be heart-breaking to spoil such a unique recording. However, as far as I can recall at the moment, what happened was this.

'We were sitting in our van, Fred and I, listening to the local feathered chorus – and very fine it is, too – when we chanced to tune in to Number One mike. What we got was evidently a conversation between a couple of very strange characters. It seemed they had just robbed the pillar-box and were examining the contents. Apparently they got what they wanted, for one of them read out part of some document with evident satisfaction. It stated that the writer of the document, whose name I forget but which is faithfully recorded, was leaving his property to his sister.'

'I am the sister,' said Matty. 'You mean, you actually heard these men reading out my brother's will before they destroyed it? Then everything is all right, after all. But how stupid of me to post it like that! I shall never forgive myself if anything goes wrong. I do hope this record of yours will be accepted as evidence of my brother's will.'

'I'm not at all sure about that.'

It was the Professor who spoke.

'Ordinarily, a mechanical recording is not accepted as evidence in a court of law. It may prove useful corroborative testimony, but a clever barrister might make things very difficult.'

Everyone was looking puzzled and anxious. The Professor turned to Humphrey.

'Let me beg you,' he said, 'to take care of the record. It will certainly be most valuable in helping to convict the criminals, once the police lay hands on them. However, let me put you all out of your suspense and explain as briefly as I can how matters stand. Miss Jay,

I must at once reassure you about your property – for there is no question that this house is your own, to do what you like with. Of that there can be no possible doubt.'

They all looked relieved, but still puzzled.

'But the will,' said Matty, 'if these men burnt the will –'

'Your brother's will, Miss Jay,' said the Professor, 'is perfectly safe. It is at this moment in the strong-room at the Southern Provincial Bank in Mulcaster. I handed it to the manager myself this morning, and I have his receipt for it in my pocket. Let me explain. But first, if I may suggest it, let us all have something to eat. The younger generation are looking decidedly hungry.'

Drinks were passed along the table, and sandwiches, buns, and cakes handed round. When everyone had something to eat, the Professor continued speaking.

'I must apologize to you, Miss Jay,' he said, 'for having become your acquaintance on false pretences. I am not a naturalist on holiday – at least, I am not much of a naturalist – I am really a sort of detective. Collecting moths and butterflies, it is true, is one of my hobbies, but my real job is that of a private in-vestigator.

'My friend the County Medical Officer told me of your proposal to give this house to the county for a chest hospital. He said that while he was touched by your generous impulse, he was afraid that the house was not really yours to give. It seemed that there was no will. However, to be on the safe side, he felt that someone should be in the neighbourhood who could keep an eye on things, and make sure that, if a will did exist, it came into the right hands. I told him that I was entitled to a bit of a holiday in the country, and that I would gladly make it a busman's holiday by keeping an eye on the Manor.'

'But why didn't you tell me?' asked Matty.

'I fancy,' answered the Professor, 'that my friend the Medical Officer did not want to make a fool of himself. He had already as good as told you he didn't think there was a will, but afterwards, it seems, he had had second thoughts and decided to be on the safe side by calling me in.

'I needn't trouble you with the whole story of what I did. Actually, I did very little. It was our excellent friends, the younger generation, who discovered the missing document. But I, you understand, was not only anxious to see that the will was safe, I wanted to bring these two particular conspirators to justice. One of them has been wanted by the police for many months for the Liverpool mail-bag robbery, and the other has also an account to settle for certain shady dealings in connexion with horse-racing.

'Our young friends very nearly upset things the other night when they discovered me catching moths by moonlight in the paddock. It so happened that the two men I was after were also at the Manor that night. It was they who got into the library with a skeleton key to the french windows and turned so many books and papers upside down. I was there keeping an eye on them. Unfortunately I could not wait to explain myself to our young friends, so they naturally concluded that I was up to no good. Next day they told you, Miss Jay, of my suspicious behaviour; then in the afternoon they found the will. I was anxious, you must remember, not only to protect this document, but also to catch the men who had been trying, unsuccessfully, to steal it.

Only by watching you carefully, to see what you did with the will, could I be sure of success. You did not post it the same evening, and next morning you were obliged, owing to the unfortunate misbehaviour of your dog, to spend some hours going to the police station in Mulcaster. I decided that no risk should be taken with the precious paper, which was not safe so long as these men were at large, even though, as I discovered, you had locked your door.

'So I thought the best thing was to do a bit of burglary myself. As you know, I had made myself familiar with the roofs and gables at "Rosebank" by climbing about them in rubber shoes in search of specimens. Your window, Miss Jay, is fortunately sheltered both from the road and from the garden. Otherwise somebody might have seen me, about eleven o'clock this very morning, hopping nimbly down into your room from the window-sill. I quickly removed the will from its hiding-place and made a copy.

'Alas for my well-laid plans! I did indeed manage to get down to Mulcaster and deliver the precious will at the bank. I then proposed, in the afternoon, to keep an eye on the thieves and try to catch them actually stealing the dummy will. But fate stepped in. Shortly after lunch a police inspector from Mulcaster turned up at "Rosebank" and ordered me to return with him to the station to answer some questions. It seems that you, Miss Jay, had reported me to the police for having been caught hanging about the grounds of the Manor by moonlight.'

'I am so sorry,' said Matty. 'It was such a stupid thing to do. But then, you know, I wasn't very well acquainted with you, and you might have been after the will yourself.'

'You did perfectly right,' said the Professor. 'My conduct looked most suspicious. You might well have thought I had been rummaging in the library. Well, the inspector from Mulcaster refused to believe me when I told him who I was. He said that was nothing to do with him, and his orders were that I was to come down to the station immediately and talk to the super-intendent. It took me a long while to persuade the superintendent that I was urgently needed in the neighbourhood of "Rosebank". It was Richard's call to the police in Mulcaster soon after four o'clock that finally settled the matter. When he rang up to say that two men had set fire to the heath, I guessed what had happened, and was able to persuade the police to lose no time in bringing me to the scene of the crime.

'Well, you all know the rest –'

The Professor was interrupted by the ringing of the telephone bell in the library. Matty went to answer it, and returned to say that it was a call for the Professor.

While he was out of the room, everyone discussed his extraordinary story, and those who had been too excited before to eat now took the opportunity of making up for lost time.

In a few minutes the Professor returned.

'You will all be glad to hear,' he announced, 'that the Mulcaster police tell me that the car described by Richard has been stopped in South Bentley. The two men have been brought back to Mulcaster to answer a charge of robbing Her Majesty's mail, and various other charges including that of administering chloro-form with intent to commit a felony. A warrant has also been issued for the arrest, in London, of Mr Gerald Jay as an accessory before the fact.'

Chapter Seventeen

HOW IT ALL ENDED

THE news spread as rapidly as the fire had spread on Mulbridge Heath. But there was no one to extinguish it – indeed, the many tongues of gossip were only too ready to fan the children's fame into a positive blaze of glory.

Humphrey and Fred, before departing for London in the recording van, had telephoned the B.B.C., and a brief reference to the capture of the two criminals was made in the nine o'clock news.

Next morning the newspapers all contained varying accounts of the day's happenings, and the children's homes, as well as 'Rosebank' Guest-House, were besieged by reporters. There were photographs of all the children, separately and together, of Matty and the Manor, even of Dennis and Dragon, upon whose weather-beaten back one newspaper reported that the Professor had pursued the criminals over the heath. Richard and Deborah were interviewed for a television news-reel. Doctor Masters and his wife, who had returned from the Broads two days before, also received a certain amount of publicity, and Doctor Masters gave an interview on the need for a new hospital in the Mulcaster area. All the publicity and excitement were not unwelcome, since no discredit attached to anyone in the neighbourhood. By the time it had died down, Winston and Deborah had gone off to London to stay for a week with an aunt and uncle, Mrs Masters had begun to pack for the long-awaited family holiday in

Wales, and Anne and Beaver, too, had gone away on their respective holidays.

Seedy and Dusty were in due course convicted of several crimes, of which the most important were described as 'administering chloroform with intent to commit a felony, robbery with violence, and stealing a postal packet'. On all except the first charge, of which he knew nothing, Gerald Jay was convicted as an accessory before the fact. All three were sentenced to long terms of imprisonment; Seedy and Dusty had both been in prison before, but Gerald had not; it need scarcely be said that he found the discomfort unwelcome in the extreme.

There was one event which none of the children missed; and that was the August number of the radio programme, 'Bird Songs of the Month'. But the feature, delightful as it was for its beautiful reproductions of the famous Mulbridge birds, contained no reference to the unique recording obtained by a lucky chance almost at the moment of the robbery. This was reserved till later.

Stephen Jay's will – the genuine one – was delivered promptly to the lawyers in London, who pondered over it for a great while; and since no one came forward to contest it, they pronounced that there was little doubt that its provisions would be declared legal. In other words, they told Matty that, after certain formalities had been completed, she could undoubtedly take possession of the Manor as her own undisputed property, to do whatever she liked with.

The County Medical Officer, apologizing handsomely to Matty for his previous attitude, said he was overjoyed to recommend to his committee the acceptance of Matty's generous offer; and the committee declared themselves in favour of taking over Mulbridge Manor for immediate conversion into a hospital for diseases of the chest and lungs.

The County Council, which had its offices and held its meetings in Mulcaster, the county town, was never in a hurry to decide on anything, particularly when this meant spending money; but they felt that now was the time to hold some sort of celebration of the remarkable events that had just transpired in the neighbourhood. An official reception was to be held at the Town Hall in the early autumn, at which the Mayor of Mulcaster was to preside, and innumerable dignitaries were to be present.

All the children and their parents were invited. The Mayor turned out in his official robes and his chain of office, and all the other officials who possessed robes were similarly bedecked.

It was an occasion which, as the *Mulcaster Gazette* asserted, 'would long be remembered with pride and gratitude in the history of the city and the county'. To describe it would be both impossible and unnecessary.

It would be pleasant to record that the day proved fine, but the weather, as often happens on even more important occasions, did not cooperate, and a thin drizzle fell nearly all day from a monotonous grey sky. But nobody minded the weather.

'I bet you're glad,' said Richard to Anne, as they took their places in the great hall.

'Yes,' said Anne. 'Our doctor says they may have the hospital ready by next summer, and he'll see that Mummy is one of the first patients to be admitted. He says a proper course of treatment in hospital is what she wants, to make her quite well again.'

'Hullo,' said Winston. 'Who's that on the platform?'

It was Miss Anstey-Farthing. She had arrived at the
Town Hall on her little motor-bike, and was now
seated among the members of the medical committee;
Matty was sitting beside her. Both ladies beamed and
waved at the children. As a friend of the County Medical Officer, the Professor, too, was on the platform;
and in the front row were Mrs Mead, Mrs Mosscrop,
accompanied by Ivy, and another hero of the hour –
the postman, Ted Hoskins, with Mrs Hoskins beside
him.

This is no place to quote the whole of His Worship
the Mayor's memorable speech. It can be read in full
in the files of the *Mulcaster Gazette*. In a great many
well-chosen words he expressed the county's sense of
pride in the generosity and enterprise of Miss Jay and
her youthful colleagues. He was able to inform his
hearers, he was happy to state, that a vacant cottage had
been found in Mulbridge suitable to Miss Jay's require-

ments, and this would be handed over to her, rent free, as a substitute for the Manor.

'It has such a nice little garden,' Matty told the children afterwards. 'Not too big for me to manage, and there will be room for Dennis too, so that he won't have to run wild and annoy the police. It's quite near "Rosebank", so I can easily go and help Mrs Mosscrop when the guest-house is full of visitors.'

The Mayor was happy to announce, also, that gifts of National Savings Certificates had been voted to all the children. 'When they were asked what they wanted,' he said, 'none of them could think of anything they were specially in need of, except a whole holiday for the schools. It is my pleasure to announce that another day will be added to the half-term holiday in all the schools throughout the county; Richard Masters attends a private preparatory school, and his headmaster – who is a good friend of mine – has also agreed to give Richard's school a holiday at the same time.'

This announcement was received with loud cheers, even the sternest parents pretending, for the occasion, that they regarded an extra holiday as a good thing.

The Mayor felt that by this time he had said enough, and there was really nothing left for him to be happy about, so amid renewed applause he sat down.

When most of the crowd had dispersed, there was a select party in the Mayor's parlour, to which all the participants in the great event were invited.

Winston, it is true, found the extremely small, triangular sandwiches quite unsatisfying, and he was obliged to circulate unobtrusively, helping himself from as many plates as possible. But everything was of the most superior quality. Cherry was so overcome by excitement that she was with difficulty persuaded to eat anything.

'Miss Jay,' asked Deborah earnestly, as soon as she had the chance to get a word with Matty, 'what is going to happen to Dragon?'

'Oh, he'll be quite all right,' said Matty. 'He's to have the use of the paddock for the rest of his life. The groundsman at the hospital will look after him.'

'I'm so glad,' said Deborah happily.

'It's all been wonderful,' said Matty to the children, who were grouped around her. 'Don't you think so?'

'Sure has,' said Winston.

'I wish it wasn't all over,' said Richard.

'Same here,' agreed Beaver, trying to make three mouthfuls of a very small chocolate éclair, for the sake of appearances.

'But it isn't all over,' said Matty. 'For me it's only just begun. You know, I want to think I've made six new friends. I do hope you'll come and see me – often. I shall move into "Lime Cottage" – that's the name of my new house – quite soon, and I want you all to come for a house-warming party. Will you?'

They agreed most heartily.

'Anne and I will be almost neighbours, won't we, my dear?'

'Yes,' said Anne, 'I'll come in and help you with the house sometimes.'

'And I'll come over and mow the lawn,' said Beaver. '*You* can't do that.'

'And I'll come and talk to you,' said Cherry.

'I can help in the garden too,' offered Winston, 'and fix up shelves and things, if you like.'

'I'll come too,' said Richard.

'And may I come and read your old children's books?' asked Deborah.

'Indeed you may,' answered Matty emphatically. 'Thank you all for everything you've done, and everything you've promised to do.'

Everyone looked forward to the house-warming party. Meanwhile, one further event was to take place.

That evening, the B.B.C. had arranged a special feature programme relating the whole story of the finding of the will and the capture of the criminals. Humphrey and Fred had been present with their apparatus at the reception in the Town Hall, and selections from the speeches were to be included; the famous recording of Seedy and Dusty reading the Professor's copy of the will was also to be broadcast.

The postman had been asked to describe his experiences; the Professor had undertaken to recount his part in the proceedings; the voices of the children, the chief of the local fire brigade, the police superintendent, the County Medical Officer, and Matty herself, had also been recorded.

It was at the Shipleys' pretty cottage that the children gathered just before eight o'clock to hear the programme. Mr and Mrs Shipley had insisted that for once Anne's friends were to be their guests. A special dispensation to stay up late had been granted, and Doctor Masters had promised to call for the Mulcaster party afterwards in his car.

Mr Shipley had lit a fire of logs in the sitting-room grate, and the light of the flames played warmly on the old, dark beams overhead, as the audience settled down happily to hear themselves on the air. A single oil-lamp lit up the faces of the children. Anne's mother sat in the rocking-chair with Cherry on her lap; her father stood beside the radio; he looked at his watch and switched on. The strains of a dance tune came from the loudspeaker. Mr Shipley adjusted the tuning knob and the volume control. The music faded, and the announcer gave the names of the dance band and its conductor.

Then the tones of another announcer were heard.

'This is the B.B.C. Light Programme,' he said. 'The time is eight o'clock. We present a special feature entitled:

MULBRIDGE MANOR
or
Where There's a Will –

This afternoon, in the historic city of Mulcaster, occurred an unusual celebration. In the ancient Town Hall were gathered . . .'

Cherry, wide-eyed, put her thumb in her mouth and determined to stay awake. The others settled down comfortably to listen.